Ellie felt her jaw tighten, turbid emotions, clashing and turbulent, sloshing inside her. If she really, truly were to do the unthinkable— agree to marry a man she barely knew—she had to be rock-solid sure she would get the protection her family needed.

"There are, as you said, terms and conditions—" She had got her brisk businesslike tone back, and was relieved she could still adopt it. "The first of which is—" she took a breath, marshaling her strength to make it crystal clear to him "—this is not going to be a long-term marriage! Two years, no more, gives you ample time to take all the social advantage you want out of marrying a princess! I won't be browbeaten on this," she emphasized. "After two years I walk away from you—completely away."

Leon's face had closed. For a second, just a second, Ellie felt a thrill of apprehension go through her. The hard planes of his face seemed harder suddenly, his dark eyes darker. Shuttered.

Then, abruptly, his expression changed. "If it makes you happy to insist on that, so be it," he murmured, giving the slightest shrug of his shoulder.

"Good," she said decisively.

Julia James lives in England and adores the peaceful verdant countryside and the wild shores of Cornwall. She also loves the Mediterranean—so rich in myth and history, with its sunbaked landscapes and olive groves, ancient ruins and azure seas. "The perfect setting for romance!" she says. "Rivaled only by the lush tropical heat of the Caribbean—palms swaying by a silver-sand beach lapped by turquoise waters... What more could lovers want?"

Books by Julia James

Harlequin Presents

Securing the Greek's Legacy
The Forbidden Touch of Sanguardo
Captivated by the Greek
A Tycoon to Be Reckoned With
A Cinderella for the Greek
Tycoon's Ring of Convenience
Billionaire's Mediterranean Proposal
Irresistible Bargain with the Greek

Secret Heirs of Billionaires

The Greek's Secret Son

Mistress to Wife

Claiming His Scandalous Love-Child
Carrying His Scandalous Heir

One Night With Consequences

Heiress's Pregnancy Scandal

Visit the Author Profile page
at Harlequin.com for more titles.

Julia James

THE GREEK'S DUTY-BOUND ROYAL BRIDE

HARLEQUIN
PRESENTS

HARLEQUIN®
PRESENTS®

Recycling programs
for this product may
not exist in your area.

ISBN-13: 978-1-335-14836-0

The Greek's Duty-Bound Royal Bride

Copyright © 2020 by Julia James

This edition published by arrangement with Harlequin Books S.A.

For questions and comments about the quality of this book,
please contact us at CustomerService@Harlequin.com.

Harlequin Enterprises ULC
22 Adelaide St. West, 40th Floor
Toronto, Ontario M5H 4E3, Canada
www.Harlequin.com

Printed in U.S.A.

THE GREEK'S DUTY-BOUND ROYAL BRIDE

For Ilona—and the cultural heritage you gave me

CHAPTER ONE

LEON DUKARIS GLANCED at the invoice on his desk and then, with an indifferent shrug of one broad shoulder, initialled the hefty sum for payment.

The Viscari St James was one of London's most expensive and exclusive hotels, and the coup that had ejected Mikal of Karylya from his Grand Duchy in the heart of central Europe had happened with lightning speed less than two weeks ago, so it was not surprising that the Grand Duke was finding it difficult to adjust his royal lifestyle to that of impoverished former ruler, with none of the wealth of his small but highly prosperous fiefdom at his disposal any longer.

It was a difficulty that suited Leon—bankrolling the Grand Duke's exile was not largesse on his part in the slightest. He gave a tight smile, accentuating the strong planes of his face and indenting the deep lines around his well-shaped mouth, sharpening the gold flecks in his eyes. It was, rather, an investment.

One that he fully intended to pay out handsomely.

His eyes darkened. Suddenly he was not seeing the expensively furnished office, towering over the City of London far below, the private domain of a billionaire and his working environment. His vision went way beyond that—way back into the past. The bitter, impoverished past…

The line for the soup kitchen in the bleak Athens winter, holes in the soles of his shoes, shivering in the cold, queuing for hot food to take back to the cramped lodging where he and his mother had to live now they'd been evicted from their spacious apartment for non-payment of rent. He is all his mother has now—the husband who professed to love her for all eternity has run out on her, abandoning her and him, their young teenage son, to the worst that the collapse of the Greek economy in the great recession over a dozen years ago can do to them…

And the worst had been bad—*very* bad—leaving them in an abject poverty that Leon had vowed he would escape, however long it took him.

And he had escaped. His success, doggedly pursued, his focus on nothing else, had lifted him rung by rung up the ladder of financial success. He had taken risks that had always paid off, even if he'd had to steel his nerves with every speculative gamble he pulled off. It had been a relentless pursuit of wealth that had seen him become a financial speculator *extraordinaire*, spotting multi-million-euro opportunities before others did and seizing them, each one taking him further up into the stratosphere of billionairedom.

But now he wanted his money to achieve something else for him. His smile widened into a tight line of satisfaction. Something that had now come within his reach, thanks to the coup in Karylya that had ousted its sovereign.

The gold glint in Leon's night-dark eyes came again at the thought. A princess bride to set the seal on his dizzying ascent from the lines for the soup kitchen.

Grand Duke Mikal's daughter.

'Ellie! There is news about your father! Bad news!'

In her head, Ellie could hear the alarm in her mother's voice, echoing still as she emerged from the tube station at Piccadilly Circus, hurrying down St James's and into the Hotel Viscari.

A stone's throw from St James's Palace, Clarence House and Buckingham Palace itself, it was often frequented by diplomats, foreign politicians and even visiting royalty.

Including deposed visiting royalty.

Deposed.

The word rang chill in Ellie's head and she felt her stomach clench. The coup causing her father and his family to flee their fairy-tale palace in Karylya had turned the Grand Duke into nothing more than a former sovereign in exile. Ellie's glance swept the Edwardian opulence of the Viscari's marbled lobby. Albeit a very luxurious exile...

She hastened up to the reception desk. 'Grand Duke Mikal's suite, please!' she exclaimed, breathless from hurrying and agitation.

'Whom shall I say?' asked the receptionist, lifting her phone.

She sounded doubtful, and Ellie could understand why. Her work-day outfit, crumpled from an overnight transatlantic flight, was more suited to the life she lived in rural Somerset with her mother and stepfather, where she had been since an infant, than to someone who had an entrée to a royal suite at a deluxe London hotel.

'Just say Lisi!' she replied, giving the Karylyan diminutive of her name.

Moments later the receptionist's attitude had changed and she was briskly summoning a bellhop. 'Escort Her Highness to the Royal Suite,' she instructed.

As she sped upwards in the elevator Ellie wished her identity had not been guessed—she never used her title anywhere outside Karylya, except on rare state occasions with her father. Instead she used the English diminutive and her British stepfather's surname—the name on her passport. Ellie Peters. It made life a lot simpler. And it was also considerably shorter than her patronym.

Elizsaveta Gisella Carolinya Augusta Feoderova Alexandreina Zsofia Turmburg-Malavic Karpardy.

She must have been named after every single aunt, grandmother and other female member of every European royal house her father claimed kin with!

From Hapsburgs to Romanovs, and any number of German royal houses, not to mention Polish, Hungarian and Lithuanian ones, and even an Ottoman or two thrown in somewhere for good measure, the nine-hundred-year-old dynasty had somehow, by luck, determination, shrewd alliances and even shrewder marriages, clung on to the mountain fastness that was the Grand Duchy of Karylya, with its high snow-capped peaks and deep verdant valleys, its dark pine forests and rushing rivers, glacial lakes and modern ski slopes.

Except now—Ellie felt her stomach clench in dismay and disbelief at the news her mother had announced—

that nine-hundred-year possession had suddenly, devastatingly, come to an end...

The elevator's polished doors slid open as the car came to a halt and Ellie stepped out into the quiet, deserted lobby of this exclusive floor of suites and residences. One of the doors opposite was flung open and a figure came hurtling through, embracing her as she hurried forward.

'Oh, Lisi, thank heavens you are here!'

It was her younger sister, Marika—her half-sister, actually, one of her two half-siblings, offspring of her father and his second wife. Although Marika was here with her parents, Ellie knew from the fractured phone call she'd made from the airport that her younger brother, Niki, her father's heir—his *former* heir, she realised now, with a start of dismayed realisation—was still at school in Switzerland, in the throes of critically important university entrance exams.

How he had taken the grim news Ellie didn't know—but Marika, as was clear from her heartfelt cry now, was not coping well.

'I can't believe this has happened!' she heard herself cry back, answering her sister in the Karylyan Marika had used.

'It's like a nightmare!' Marika said, drawing Ellie into the suite.

'How is Papa?' Ellie asked, her voice sombre.

'Shell-shocked. He can't take it in. No more can Mutti—' Marika gave a shuddering sigh. 'Come on... come in. Papa's been waiting and waiting for you.'

Ellie hurried forward into the spacious reception room beyond the suite's hallway. Absently, she took in the luxury of the place—though, of course, compared with the palace it was nothing at all…

Inside, she saw the room was crowded—her father, his wife the Grand Duchess, and several of the palace staff were there. Her father was standing immobile by the plate glass window that opened on to a private terrace, staring out over the rooftops. He turned as Ellie came in, and instinctively she rushed to hug him.

A sharp voice stilled her. '*Elizsaveta!* You forget yourself!'

It was the Grand Duchess, her stepmother, admonishing her. Realising what she was being called to do, she took a breath, dropping an awkward curtsy in her knee-length skirt. But as she did so she felt her stomach hollowing. Her father was no longer a reigning sovereign…

He came forward now, to take her hands and press them in his cold ones. 'You finally came,' he said. There was both relief and a tinge of criticism in his tone.

Ellie swallowed. 'I'm sorry, Papa—we were in Canada…far in the north. Filming with Malcolm. Communication was difficult, we were so remote, and then I had to get back here and—'

She stopped. In the disaster that had befallen him her father would hardly be concerned about her mother and her stepfather, a distinguished wildlife documentary filmmaker, whose work took him all over the world and for whom her mother had left her royal husband when Ellie had been only a baby.

'Well, you are here now, thankfully,' her father said, his voice warmer. Then he turned to one of the nearby members of staff. 'Josef—refreshments!' he commanded.

Ellie bit her lip. She'd always believed her father's stiffly imperious manner had contributed to his growing unpopularity in Karylya. And her unspoken thoughts had been echoed in all the political analyses she had read since the news had broken, giving the reasons for the coup.

That and his intransigent refusal to entertain any degree of constitutional, fiscal or social reform in order to defuse the potentially toxic and historically fraught ethnic mix of the population, whose internecine rivalries had always required careful and constant balancing against each other to prevent any one minority feeling slighted and ignored.

Ellie sighed inwardly. The trouble was her father lacked the astute political management skills and charismatic, outgoing personality of his own father. Grand Duke Nikolai had successfully steered Karylya through the diplomatic minefield of the Iron Curtain decades, maintaining the duchy's precarious independence against huge foreign pressures and gaining the great prosperity the duchy now enjoyed. Her father's reserve and awkwardness had, in the ten years of his reign, only managed to alienate every faction—even those traditionally most supportive of him.

Which had left none to support him when the coup, led from the High Council by the leader of the ethnic faction with the strongest perceived grievances, had erupted.

Now her father and his Grand Duchess were harbouring a deep and, she allowed, understandable anger and resentment at their fate. It was evident in their condemnation of all who had contributed to their ignominious flight. For her part, Ellie merely murmured sympathetically—it was obvious her father and stepmother needed to vent their understandably strong emotions. More rational discussion could take place later—she hoped. And all the awkward questions could be asked later, too.

Finally taking refuge in Marika's bedroom, Ellie asked the question which was most concerning her, which she could not possibly have asked in front of any member of the remaining royal staff, however loyal they were.

'Marika, what's happening about Papa's finances? What has the new government agreed to? It must have been quite a generous settlement...' She glanced around her at the luxuriously appointed bedroom. 'This place doesn't come cheap, that's for sure!'

But her sister was looking at her with an expression that struck a chill through her. And her features were strained.

'Papa isn't paying for this hotel, Lisi! He can't afford it—oh, Lisi, he can't afford anything at all! We're completely penniless!'

The blood drained from Ellie's face. 'Penniless?' she echoed in a hollow voice.

Her sister nodded, her features still contorted. 'He's been told by the new head of government that he won't get any kind of financial settlement at all, and that all the royal assets have been frozen!'

'*Nothing?*' Ellie gasped disbelievingly. Then her eyes went around the luxuriously appointed bedroom again. 'But...but this place...? You've been here nearly a fortnight already...'

Consternation was flooding through her as Marika's

expression changed. Now awkwardness was vivid in her pretty features.

'Like I said, Lisi… Papa isn't paying for this suite— someone else is.'

Ellie stared, dismay filling her like cold water. 'But *who*?' she demanded.

Marika's answer was fractured and disjointed. 'He's called Leon—Leon Dukaris—and he's a billionaire— Greek. He was in Karylya last summer, on business. He came to the summer opera gala that Mutti is patroness for. He was introduced to us—and Papa invited him to a garden party at the palace. Then he came to a reception and a dinner, too—I didn't really pay any attention. It was a business affair with some of the ministers and other foreign investors. He was mostly talking to them and Papa. I… I don't really know much more, except that when we arrived in London he got in touch with Papa and told him he would underwrite our expenses…'

Ellie was still staring. 'But *why*? Why should this… this Leon Dukaris care about Papa? Let alone fork out for this place! If he wants to do business in Karylya it's not Papa he should be making up to,' she finished bitterly.

A tide of colour washed up her sister's face, and something about Marika's expression curdled Ellie's blood.

'Marika, what is it?' she asked urgently.

Her sister was twisting her hands, a look of anguish in her face. 'Oh, God, Lisi—there's only one reason he's paying for everything! He wants…' She swallowed. 'He wants to marry me!'

Ellie's eyes widened in total disbelief. '*Marry* you? You can't be serious!'

'He's making it obvious!' Marika cried. 'He's been here several times, always very attentive to me. Way more than just being polite! I do my best to put him off, but I know Mutti is hoping I'll encourage him. She's worried sick about what's going to happen to us now, and if he really wants to marry me—'

She broke off, her voice choking. Ellie's dismay doubled. It was bad enough learning that her father was penniless, and that he was being bankrolled by some unknown Greek billionaire…but that her sister should believe the Greek billionaire wanted to *marry* her…?

Surely Marika was imagining it? Upset and overwrought as she so obviously was right now by the disaster that had befallen their family?

In a macabre attempt at humour, at a time when humour was absolutely impossible, Ellie heard herself blurt out, 'Just please don't tell me that this Leon Dukaris is some creepy, lecherous old man with a fat gut and piggy eyes!'

'No, not exactly,' Marika answered in a shaky voice. But then her eyes welled with tears. 'Oh, Lisi, it doesn't matter what he looks like or who he is!' Her tears spilled over into open weeping. 'I'm in love with someone else!' she cried. 'So I can't marry Leon Dukaris! I just *can't*!'

Leon vaulted from his limo, now drawn up in the entrance sweep of the Viscari St James, and strode into the lobby. It was time to visit the royal family again.

He had called upon the Grand Duke several times since his abrupt arrival in London two weeks ago—

ostensibly to give him his assurance that all his expenses would be underwritten by himself for the duration of his stay, until such time as he had decided where to live out his exile and do whatever it was that former monarchs did when their countries no longer wanted them. But the real reason for his visits was quite different.

He was trying to decide whether he was truly going to go ahead with claiming a princess for his bride—the ultimate prize.

Thoughts played across his mind as the elevator doors to the penthouse floor slid shut. Was he simply being fanciful in even giving house room to the idea? It had come to him the previous summer, when he had been visiting Karylya on business, being invited to the palace, socialising with the royal family, meeting Princess Marika…

At the time he had given it no serious thought, but the idea had grown on him during the intervening months. The girl, though a brunette, and quiet in her manner, was very pretty, and if his own tastes actually ran to blondes—well, for the sake of a princess bride surely he could change his tastes…

Nor was she unintelligent, from what he could judge of her, and that was another key advantage. His features hardened momentarily. So was the crucial fact that, as a princess, she'd be perfectly open to the idea of marrying for practical reasons. Love—his mouth tightened— would not get to taint their marriage…

He snapped his mind away from his darkening thoughts. No, there was nothing to rule Princess Marika out of his consideration…and now that events had taken such a disastrous turn for the Karylyan royal family, from the princess's point of view—and her parents'—there was every incentive for her to consider his proposal seriously.

If he were to make one, of course…

But should I?

That his suit would be favoured by her parents was obvious—what could be more desirable than a very wealthy son-in-law to keep on bankrolling their exile indefinitely? As for the princess herself… He knew without vanity that he was highly attractive to women—his life, even while he had still been in the process of making his huge fortune, had been filled with eager females demonstrating that undeniable fact to him. Now, in his thirties, he was done playing the field. He would be perfectly happy to settle down with one agreeable female and he would make the princess a good husband.

And theirs would be an honest marriage. He wouldn't delude and deceive his bride with hypocritical declarations of undying love and endless mouthing of romantic flummery that meant nothing when the chips were down.

Leon's dark eyes hardened with harsh memory. His father had made such endless declarations—Leon had grown up hearing him telling his mother how devoted he was to her, how much he loved her, how she meant the world to him, how she was the moon and the stars and all the other romantic verbiage he had lavished upon her.

It had counted for *nothing*.

When the Greek economy had crashed his father had taken off with another woman—conveniently wealthy—

leaving his heartbroken wife and his teenage son to cope on their own. Abandoning them totally.

His mother had been devastated by the betrayal—Leon had been only angry. Deeply, bitterly angry. And contemptuous of the man who had abandoned them.

I will never be like him—never! I will never do to a woman what my father did to my mother! Because I will never tell a woman I love her. Because I will never fall in love. Because love doesn't exist—only meaningless words that lie...and destroy.

The elevator glided to a halt, the doors sliding open, and Leon shook his dark memories from him. The miseries of his teenage years were gone and he would not be haunted by them. He had made his life on his own terms—and those were the terms he would make any marriage on. Terms that would never include what did not exist—would never include love...

His wife, when he married—whoever she was, princess or not—would get respect, regard, friendship and companionship.

And, of course, desire. That went without saying...

It was a word he should not have admitted into his thoughts at that moment. Because as he strode out of the elevator the door to the royal suite opened and a woman emerged.

Instinctively his eyes took her in, in one comprehensive sweep.

Tall, blonde, slender, with grey-blue eyes and her hair caught back in a ponytail. Not wearing any make-up. Her clothes non-descript—certainly not couture or designer. Yet that didn't matter in the least. Because she was, without doubt, breathtakingly, stunningly beautiful... Instantly desirable.

He felt a rush of adrenaline quicken in his bloodstream.

Who is she?

He had never seen her before—no woman that stunning would have escaped his eye.

He realised she was gazing at him, stopped in her tracks just as he was. For a moment—an enjoyably adrenaline-fuelled moment—Leon allowed himself the pleasure of meeting her gaze full-on, letting her see just how pleasurable it was for him to look at her...

Then, abruptly, her eyes peeled away from his and he saw colour flare across her high-cut cheekbones. Dipping her head, she hurried forward, veering around him to dive into the waiting elevator behind him. He gave a low laugh. Whoever she was, if she had joined the entourage of the Grand Duke, in whatever capacity, he would at some point see her again. And that would suit him very well...

His thoughts cut out. Realisation slammed into him. Hell, no, it would *not* suit him to see the breathtaking blonde again!

Taking an incised breath, he strode forward again, heading for the door of the royal suite. The breathtaking blonde, whoever she was, could be no concern of his. He had a princess to woo...

CHAPTER TWO

ELLIE SLUMPED BACK against the wall of the elevator car, feeling weak. Her heart was thumping like a sledge-hammer. *Oh, sweet heaven, what had just happened?*

She had issued from her father's suite and, without the slightest warning that it was about to happen, had all but rushed right into the most devastating male she had ever set eyes on in her life...

Talk about tall, dark and handsome!

She felt weakness flush through her again, her heart-rate quicken. It had lasted only a handful of moments—a silent gasp from her, a sweep of night-dark eyes. That was all she'd needed to take in his Savile-Row-tailoring, his six-foot-plus height, broad shoulders and lean hips, his planed features... And those night-dark eyes, look-ing her over, liking what he was seeing, making no se-cret of it.

She shook her head angrily, as if to dissipate the after-burn on her retinas. Oh, what did it matter who that man had been? She had far more important things to think about.

Disbelief was still uppermost—surely her sister was just imagining what she'd told her? That some unknown

Greek billionaire thought he could marry her? It was outrageous—just outrageous!

She's upset, that's all. Upset, shocked and distraught after what has happened.

And then she remembered what Marika had gone on to say.

'I'm in love with someone else!'

Ellie heard her sister's tearful voice as the elevator plummeted to ground level. And when she'd learned just who it was that Marika was in love with, her heart had sunk yet further.

A man Marika's parents would never allow her to marry...

Leon was bowing over the Grand Duchess's regally outstretched hand.

'Herr Dukaris.' She smiled with an air of stately graciousness, her Germanic accent courtesy of her long lineage of Austrian aristocracy.

'Highness...' Leon intoned dutifully, having already made a brief bow to the Grand Duke.

He himself did not stand on ceremony, but what was the point of paying the exorbitant bills of European royalty if he did not acknowledge royal protocol? After all, either they were royal, and marrying into their family would set the glittering seal on his worldly success, or they were simply penniless refugees in a turbulent world, seeking a new life in a less troubled spot.

His eyes went to the royal couple's daughter. She looked drawn and anxious, and Leon could understand why. Two weeks ago she'd been a princess in a fairy-tale castle in a fairy-tale realm—now she was just a penniless young woman with no prospects other than those an accident of birth had conferred upon her.

Well, if he did marry her, her fortunes would be restored and she would smile again.

He let his gaze rest on the princess with a warmth he hoped she might find encouraging. She was, he acknowledged, very attractive in her own way, with soft features and dark eyes, dark hair and a tender mouth. Yet before he could stop himself memory flashed in his head of that fleeting encounter just now in the penthouse lobby. Now, if that stunning blonde had been the woman now sitting beside the graciously smiling Grand Duchess...

He tore his inappropriate thoughts away again, warming his smile for Princess Marika. But she remained stubbornly woebegone, as if his smiling alarmed her. He gave an inward frown. But then the Grand Duke was relating, with understandable *schadenfreude*, how the new regime in his homeland was having difficulty getting endorsement from other governments.

'Perhaps when there has been an election, as promised?' Leon ventured.

It was the wrong thing to say.

A snort came from the Grand Duke. 'A stage-managed, propaganda-fuelled plebiscite in order to elect a dictator! That's all it will be!'

Leon made no reply. Like too many small countries in that highly volatile area of Europe, Karylya was a complicated cocktail of historic rivalries that still ran deep, despite the duchy's new prosperity as a financial hub for the emerging economies of the former Eastern Bloc. 'The Luxembourg of Central Europe'—that was the way the country was usually described, which was why he'd visited the place last summer.

And thereby made the personal acquaintance of the royal family and the princess…

His eyes rested on her now, their expression veiled, his thoughts inward. Was he seriously thinking of marrying Princess Marika?

Again the image of that breathtaking blonde out in the lobby fleeted across his consciousness. How could he be considering marriage to one woman if he was still capable of having his attention caught by another one?

Wariness filled him suddenly. Though he would never declare love for a woman, he would never be disloyal to any woman he married. Not like his despised father.

Where his father was now, he had no idea—and he did not want to know. His boyish idealisation of his father, his wanting only to grow up like him, had crashed and burnt to ashes the day he'd deserted him and his mother. His father had put his own selfish interests first, abandoning his heartbroken wife, making a mockery of all those endless romantic declarations of eternal love—and abandoning his own son, betraying his paternal responsibility towards him. Thinking only of himself.

He dragged his thoughts back to the present. Whatever he decided to do now, he must not, out of decency, lead the princess or her parents to hope he would offer for her and then not.

I have to decide.

But to decide meant getting to know her better—and that, after all, was what he was doing here in the Grand Duke's suite.

'I was wondering, Highness,' he said now, addressing Princess Marika's mother, 'knowing your love of the opera, whether you might permit me to invite you to Covent Garden tonight? It is very short notice, and I apologise, but Torelli is to sing *Turandot*—and I recall from last summer that you hold her in some admiration.'

'Turandot!' exclaimed the Grand Duchess promptly. She bestowed her gracious smile upon Leon. 'How very kind. It will help to divert my daughter at this distressing time—will it not, Marika?'

The princess managed a smile, albeit a wan one.

'Then I will make the arrangements,' Leon said.

He would hardly get Princess Marika to himself, but it would be a start, and being seen conspicuously in public with the Karylyan royal family would begin the process of associating himself with them. And, of course, he added cynically, them with him.

Satisfied, he took his leave. Only as he headed back towards the elevator did he find himself wondering, yet again, just who that breathtaking blonde had been. And trying not to wonder whether he would ever see her again. Trying not to *want* to see her again...

Sternly he admonished himself.

I'm here to marry a princess—not have my head turned by another woman!

Like it or not, he had better remember that.

Ellie was hurrying again—this time into the foyer of Covent Garden's Royal Opera House. It was difficult in high heels and a full-length gown. Unlike her mother, who relished no longer having to meet the formal dress codes required of her when she had been Grand Duchess, Ellie's stepmother had insisted on evening dress tonight.

'It was quite bad enough you arriving the way you did, dressed like some sort of servant! It's out of the question that you should not remember your position from now on. Especially now.'

The Grand Duchess had said no more, but Ellie had got the message.

Especially now that her father had been deposed and sent into exile...

Well, she'd done her best this evening, but her couture wardrobe had not made it out of Karylya with her father, and all she'd had on hand at Malcolm's London flat was the outfit she'd worn to the last TV awards bash she'd attended with her mother and stepfather.

Much to Ellie's relief, her father had agreed she could stay there, since the suite at the Viscari was already crowded, and it would have required taking yet another room, running up yet another hefty bill.

The pale blue evening gown was perfectly respectable, but it was not couture, and since her Karylyan jewellery had also not made it out of the duchy and into exile, she was wearing only a pearl necklace of her mother's. She'd dressed her hair simply, applied her make-up likewise, and she knew perfectly well that no one would take her for a princess just by looking at her.

No more than that man did in the penthouse lobby.

She pushed the memory out of her head. Pointless to remember it—pointless to think about the man. Even more pointless to remember her inability to tear her eyes from him... No, it was far more important to focus on this evening.

Marika's text had elaborated on her stepmother's summons.

Lisi—you must come! Leon Dukaris will be there. Please, please, please try and keep him away from me!

Ellie's expression grew grimmer as she gained the almost deserted lobby. The performance was about to begin. She would do her very best to keep Marika's unwanted suitor from her, but her thoughts were troubled all the same as she was hurriedly shown up to the Dress Circle. For all that the man her sister had fallen in love with was someone utterly impossible for her to marry, Ellie had nothing but sympathy for Marika.

Of course Marika wanted only to marry for love!

Just as I do—and always have done!

In this day and age, after all, even a princess was allowed to believe in marrying for love…

Her face clouded. It was all very well believing that, and all very well trying to protect her sister from an unwanted suitor—but this unknown billionaire was all that stood between her father and penury. It was a sobering and unwelcome thought…

The house lights were already dimming as she was shown into the box reserved for them, and as they dimmed she made out the regal figures of her father and stepmother, already seated, another masculine figure silhouetted beside them, and beside him the slight figure of her sister.

Marika turned a grateful glance on Ellie as she hurriedly sketched a cursory curtsy to the Grand Duchess, who had thrown her an admonitory stare at her late arrival, before sitting down on the nearest chair, just behind her sister.

Busying herself with easing her skirts as she sat down, she dipped her head to smooth the fabric, missing the turning of the head of the masculine figure beside her sister until she raised her eyes, just as the conductor lifted his baton and the curtain rose on the opening scene of *Turandot*. But as she did so Ellie froze. The breath stilled in her lungs and her lips parted in shock.

The man who'd turned his head to see who was arriving so late was the same man who'd been crossing the penthouse suite lobby that afternoon. The man she had not been able to tear her eyes from.

She gave an audible gasp—she was sure of it—and for the slightest second it seemed she met that dark gaze again, head-on. Then, still in shock, she twisted her head so that her eyes were doggedly on the stage below. But she was sure that colour had run up into her cheeks and her heartbeat had grown ragged—and not just from the rush of getting here!

This was the unknown Greek—the nouveau riche billionaire bankrolling her father and setting his sights on her sister?

Her own words to Marika that morning replayed in her head now, as the opening scene of the opera got underway below her.

Old, fat and piggy-eyed...

She wanted to give a semi-hysterical choke—dear Lord, she couldn't have been further from the truth!

What had Marika said? She racked her brain to recall her sister's reply to her dismayed exclamation.

'Not exactly...'

The hysterical flutter came again—no, *definitely* 'not exactly'!

In fact, he was whatever was the total and absolute opposite of her scathing description.

She felt a rush go through her that was nothing to do with her hurried arrival and everything to do with the man sitting just in front of her. Her heart thumping in her chest, she thanked heaven she had the duration of the first act of the opera to recover her composure. Time, more importantly, to dwell on what Marika had told her.

It doesn't matter that he's like every woman's fantasy male—he can't seriously think he can marry Marika just like that! She must be imagining it—she must!

But then why was Leon Dukaris bothering to pick up the sky-high tab for her father's hotel bill? What did he think was in it for him by doing so?

Cold chilled through her veins. Her eyes rested on him now—on the broad back, the well-shaped head silhouetted against the bright lights of the stage, where the main characters were singing their hearts out, completely ignored by her right now, for there was a drama going on right here in this box that outweighed anything going on down there on the stage…

She could see he'd crossed one long leg over the other, in a kind of negligent pose, and from her angle behind him she could make out half his profile. Apparently he was focused on the stage, but she fancied he was not particularly riveted by the scene or the singing.

She could see a square-palmed hand resting on one powerful thigh, the other laxly holding a programme. There was something about the way he was sitting that made her realise his body was very slightly inclined towards her sister, as if to indicate a nascent intimacy with her, making himself at ease in her body space.

An ease that was being entirely repudiated by her sister.

Marika was, Ellie could see, sitting ramrod-straight, tension in every line of her slight body. With a tightening of her mouth, she dragged her eyes away from her sister and the man beside her, back down on to the stage—where, she realised with a belated start of realisation, a princess was vowing never to marry and her unwanted suitor was determined she should do just that...

It mustn't happen—it just mustn't!

The words formed in Ellie's head and it was not the drama on the stage that she meant.

Leon let his gaze rest on the stage below, but all he was aware of was the woman sitting behind him. He still could not believe it. She was the breathtaking female who'd stopped him in his tracks that afternoon.

Who is she?

The question burned for an answer, but the best he could come up with, having taken her in at a single brief glance, was that she was some kind of lady-in-waiting. She'd dropped a curtsy to the Grand Duchess, who'd frowned at her, and the gown she was wearing was no couture number, like the duchess's and the princess's. So, yes...lady-in-waiting would be the most likely role, wouldn't it?

He could feel emotions conflicting within him—his overpowering visceral reaction to her clashing totally with his purpose to make Princess Marika his bride. This blonde might be a fatal distraction. He was feeling that distraction even now, fighting the urge to turn and look at her.

It seemed to take for ever before the curtain finally fell on the first act, to tumultuous applause, but suddenly the Grand Duchess was addressing him as the house lights came up.

'Torelli is in perfect voice!' she exclaimed approvingly.

'Outstanding!' Leon heard himself agree politely.

Then, forcing himself, he smiled at the princess beside him, who was still looking as stiff as she had all through the first act. Leon wished she would relax a little more.

'What did you think?' he asked in a kindly tone that he hoped was encouraging.

'She was very good,' Princess Marika said faintly.

Grand Duke Mikal was getting to his feet. 'It was a damned long first act!' he exclaimed.

Leon, who privately agreed, only gave a light laugh, getting to his feet as well. No sitting when royalty stood, he made himself remember. The Duchess was remaining seated, as was her daughter, but behind him Leon could hear the blonde lady-in-waiting standing up, with a slight rustle of her skirts.

Taking it as a signal, Leon finally allowed himself to turn, feeling it like the release of a bowstring drawn too tight to bear the tension much longer.

And there she was.

He felt his blood surge again as his eyes latched on

to her. She was not looking at him, but he did not care. Was content just to drink her in.

She was as breathtakingly, stunningly beautiful as she'd been that first moment—even more so. She was wearing make-up now, enough to accentuate her eyes and mouth, to sculpt her cheekbones, and her hair was in a simple but elegant pleat. Her only jewellery was a single row of pearls, which added to the translucence of her fair skin. The style of the pale blue gown, albeit non-couture, complemented her slender beauty with its plissé bodice, cap sleeves and narrow skirt.

He felt desire, raw and insistent, spike through him. He tried to fight it back, knowing he should not indulge it—not if he was seriously considering marriage to Princess Marika.

But how can I think of such a thing when I'm reacting to another woman like this? Impossible! Just impossible!

As impossible, he recognised with a plunging realisation, as seeking to have anything to do with this unknown lady-in-waiting—even if he were to abandon the whole idea of marrying the Grand Duke's daughter. Any such liaison would be out of the question for Their Highnesses...

Frustration bit at him from every side, but still he could not tear his eyes from her. Not yet—and not when, even though she was still not looking at him, he could tell with every masculine instinct that she was acutely aware of him, responding to him as strongly as he was to her, just as she had in their initial brief encounter in the penthouse lobby.

He wanted her to look at him, but behind him he

heard the Grand Duke step forward, and the blonde dropped him a slight curtsy, murmuring something in Karylyan that Leon took to be an apology for her late arrival.

The Grand Duke said something admonitory, then turned to Leon. 'You must allow me, Dukaris,' the Grand Duke announced in English, in his heavy, formal manner, 'to make another introduction to you.'

He paused, and Leon could not deny himself the veiled pleasure of letting his eyes go back to the blonde, because that was the only place he wanted his gaze to go. Back to feast on her pale, fine-sculpted beauty, her slender, full-breasted form. He wanted to breathe in the elusive, haunting scent of her perfume…even if she could never be his…

She was standing very stiffly, still not looking his way, but a tell-tale pulse was beating at her throat.

Then the Grand Duke was speaking again, the formality of his style even more pronounced. 'My elder daughter,' he was saying now, 'the Princess Elizsaveta.'

CHAPTER THREE

LEON FELT HIS expression freeze. Felt everything in him freeze. Then, like a sudden thaw across a frozen lake, he felt everything *un*-freeze—melt into the wash of sheer, gratifying release of every last fragment of the frustration he'd felt just a few moments ago.

He felt his features lighten—everything inside him lighten. Because everything now was just *perfect*.

As perfect as she is!

His eyes rested on her, his gaze brilliant.

'Princess...'

He heard his voice husky on her title. Without conscious awareness he reached for one of her hands, saw her eyes flare as he did so, and her lips part as if she was taking in an urgent breath of air.

Then, with absolute deliberation, Leon raised her hand to his mouth and gave the slightest bow of his head. With the same absolute deliberation he let his lips brush the back of her hand, infinitely lightly. He felt it tremble in his.

He relinquished her hand, letting his glance linger on her. He heard her murmur his name—a low 'Mr Dukaris...' that was even fainter than her sister's voice.

But Leon could see the colour flaring out along those delicate cheekbones, and that was enough for him. And he saw the speed with which she had clasped the hand he'd just kissed, as if to stop it trembling.

Satisfaction filled him. And something much, much more than satisfaction.

He turned his head now to his guests, the Duke and Duchess. His smile flashed broadly. 'Champagne?' he invited.

Expansively he gestured towards the back of the box, where the requisite bottles were nestling in their ice buckets by a little table holding flutes on a silvered tray.

Champagne was exactly what was needed now. He'd never been more sure of that in his life.

Ellie was trying to hold on to the shreds of her composure—but it was impossible, just impossible! She should be used to hand-kissing—it was nothing out of the ordinary in Karylya for a female royal. Old-fashioned, perhaps, and somewhat formal as a deferential greeting. But nothing to set her fighting for composure the way she was now.

But then, never had a man as outrageously attractive as Leon Dukaris kissed her hand.

She gave a silent gulp, hoping her colour had returned to normal.

'Princess…?'

Their host for the evening, who was paying for the champagne he was now offering her with a polite smile, who was paying for this box at the opera—she dreaded to think how expensive that was—who was paying for the astronomically expensive suite at the Viscari St

James, and paying for Ellie dared not think how much more, was standing in front of her, holding a flute brimming with gently beading champagne.

She took it, murmuring her thanks and adopting an expression of extreme graciousness that would have befitted her ultra-gracious regal stepmother. It gave her the protection she urgently needed. She took a sip from the flute, hearing Leon Dukaris speak again, asking her if she was enjoying the opera. His English was accented, she noted, but not much—less so than her father's.

There was a slight smile on his mouth—beautifully sculpted, with deep lines incised around it—and she felt another silent hollowing of her stomach. The planes of his face were strong, his nose bladed, his jaw edged. There was a toughness, a determination, underlying the relaxed slanting smile that invited her to respond to his conversational gambit.

'Torelli is as outstanding as ever,' she replied, echoing her stepmother's viewpoint readily enough, 'but the role is hardly endearing. *Turandot* can't be anyone's favourite heroine.'

She was making small talk, nothing more, and had done so a thousand times in Karylya when in princess mode.

She saw a faint frown on Leon Dukaris's face.

'No? But she's a very strong woman,' he replied. 'Insisting on not marrying just because that's what everyone expects her to do.'

Ellie felt her face harden. 'Strong? She's brutal! She has her suitors murdered and her rival tortured!' she bit out.

His rejoinder was immediate. 'The slave girl, Liu,

could have avoided her fate any time she wanted, simply by telling Turandot the name of the unknown Prince.' There was a sardonic note in his voice.

'Whom Turandot would then have had killed!' Ellie shot back. 'Liu refuses to betray him—she *loves* him!'

Leon Dukaris lifted his flute to his mouth, taking a mouthful of champagne before he answered her. 'Much good it does her—he rejects her for another woman who's a better proposition than a mere slave girl!'

That sardonic note was more pronounced—harder. With something underlying it that for a moment Ellie wondered at. Then she realised that she suddenly had an opening to move the conversation away from a fictitious drama to the reality that she and her family were facing—a reality she must confront, for there was no other option but to do so if she were to protect Marika from an unwanted suitor.

'Well, yes,' she murmured, taking a sip of her champagne, pitching her voice carefully, 'Turandot is a princess—and there are, indeed, men who would like to marry a princess…'

She let her eyes rest on Leon Dukaris, mindful of her expression, nervous after her impetuosity in making so pointed an observation. Would it draw him out—make him say something that could give her any indication at all as to whether Marika's fears were justified or not?

Almost immediately, his expression was veiled. She saw his long lashes—ridiculously long lashes, inky dark and lush, she found herself noting with complete irrelevance—dipping down over those amazing dark eyes of his, tautening the muscles of her stomach.

'Well, that depends…' he replied.

And now there was no trace of any sardonic note in his voice—rather, she realised, with another pull on her heightened awareness of him, a trace of amusement… and, more than amusement, a sensual drawl that did things to her they should not…*must* not.

'On the princess in question…'

'Indeed,' she returned. 'And therefore perhaps you should be aware, Mr Dukaris, that my sister is in love with another man.'

She spoke in a low voice, for only him to hear. But even as she spoke she feared she had said too much—assumed too much.

What if Marika's fears were entirely groundless, the product of fear and distress? Well, it was too late now. She'd all but warned off Leon Dukaris from getting any ideas about her sister—ideas he might never have entertained in the first place.

It took all her training to keep her expression composed, as if she had said nothing out of the ordinary at all.

For a moment nothing changed in his expression. Then, as tension clawed in her, she saw his stance ease, a wash of relaxation go through him, and in his dark, dark eyes glints of sheer gold suddenly gleamed like buried treasure.

He raised his flute and quite deliberately tilted it to touch hers with a crystalline click of glass.

'I wish her as well as can be expected,' he said.

There was a carelessness in his voice, and again that underlying sardonic note that Ellie had heard before but had no time now to pay any attention to. For now all she had attention for was the way his eyes were holding hers, the expression in them, the way she could not move in the slightest.

'But I fear you have misunderstood the situation, Princess. I have not the slightest interest in your sister.'

He paused, and in that pause she could not breathe, for Leon Dukaris was dominating her body space, dominating her consciousness, smiling down at her with that smile that was not a smile, that smile that had nothing to do with humour in the least and everything to do with the complete lack of breath in her lungs and the bonelessness of her limbs, the hot rush of blood to her body.

'I would far prefer,' he said, and there was a sudden intimacy in the way he spoke to her, a sudden huskiness in his voice that weakened her boneless limbs, '*you* to be my bride...'

He touched his glass once more to hers. Raised it to his mouth and, smiling still, drank from it. Then, as if he had said nothing more to her than that he hoped she would enjoy the evening, despite disliking the heroine of the opera, he turned and strolled towards his other guests.

Behind him, Ellie felt her cheeks burst into flame, and the hand holding her champagne flute shook.

He couldn't have just said what he had.

He couldn't!

But he had.

She waited to feel the outrage she surely must feel— but it did not come. And she could only stare after him, motionless, hearing his outrageous words echoing in her head.

Leon stood by the plate glass picture window of the apartment above his offices. It was his London pied-àterre, and furnished in ultra-modern, ultra-expensive style by top interior designers. He did not care for it, but it was prestigious enough for the business entertaining he did—and from time to time for the personal entertaining of those women he selected for the interludes in his life which had punctuated the years of his adulthood.

He made it crystal-clear to each and every woman that their affair would be brief, would be a passing mutual, sensual pleasure—nothing more. Never would he deceive any woman and pretend that he was offering any more than that.

His thoughts flickered as he took a meditative mouthful of cognac, staring out unseeing over the City skyline, glittering like jewels in the night at this late hour.

He was done with this lifestyle. Of that he was sure. It had served its purpose over the years of accumulating his vast wealth, but it had run its course. He wanted something different now.

Some*one* different.

His expression changed. How had it happened? That extraordinary confluence of two quite separate desires? The fanciful notion that had beguiled him last year in the fairy-tale Grand Duchy of Karylya, that he could crown his achievements with the most glittering prize of all—a royal bride... Then encountering a woman who, in his very first glimpse of her, had set his senses afire in an indelible instant—and then, in a veritable gift from the gods, to discover that she might be the royal bride he sought...

The woman I desire and the princess I aspire to marry—one and the same... The alluringly beautiful Princess Elizsaveta.

Dismissing the lovelorn Princess Marika from his thoughts for ever, he let the syllables of her older sister's name linger in his head, let memory replay every moment of their encounter, their conversation. He did not mind that he had declared his hand—he welcomed the opportunity she'd given him to do so. It cut to the chase—made things crystal-clear.

She was the princess bride he wanted.

Now all that remained was for her to agree...

And why should she not?

A slow, sensual smile pulled at his mouth, and his eyes glinted gold with reminiscence. The breathtaking blonde who had so incredibly fortuitously turned out to be a princess had not been able to hide from him the fact that she returned his attraction—her responsiveness to him had blazed in every glance, in her shimmering awareness of him as a man.

She desires me even as I desire her.

And added to that desire, which curled even now, seductive and sensual through his bloodstream, all the worldly advantages that would accrue with their marriage, for both of them—how could there be any argument against it?

It was the perfect match.

And, best of all, both of us will know the reasons we are marrying—and that the meaningless charade of 'love' has nothing to do with it!

And never would.

He lifted his cognac glass, toasting the one and only royal bride he wanted—the beautiful, the breathtaking Princess Elizsaveta.

* * *

The week that followed was the most tormented of Ellie's life. Her head ached with it. Had Leon Dukaris really meant what he'd so outrageously declared at the opera? Or had it been only a flippant remark in riposte to her warning him off Marika? *If* he'd actually needed warning off?

But if he wasn't entertaining such ambitions, then why was he forking out a fortune on keeping her family in horrendously expensive luxury?

His intentions remained impossible to determine.

When he invited the royal family to luncheon, two days after the evening at Covent Garden, to be taken in a *salon privé* at the hotel, she could detect nothing in his manner beyond formal civility. For herself, though she called on her training in royal etiquette to remain outwardly composed, it was a quite different matter.

The visceral impact Leon Dukaris made on her the moment he entered the room had strengthened, not lessened—she was even more hopelessly aware of him than ever—and it was the same yet again when, the day after, he took herself and Marika to afternoon tea at Meredon, her stepmother having graciously approved the outing for her confined daughter.

As they sat on the terrace of the ultra-prestigious country house hotel just outside London, overlooking the green sward stretching down to the River Thames, Ellie was burningly conscious of their host. Doggedly, she pursued safe conversational topics—from the history of the politically powerful Georgian family who had once owned Meredon to the flood protection measures needed for the River Thames in a warming world.

Marika was little help, merely picking at the delicious teatime fancies while staring off forlornly into the distance.

For his part Leon Dukaris, sporting a pair of ultra-fashionable designer shades that made him look even more devastatingly attractive than ever, kept the conversation going by asking lazily pertinent questions and giving the impression that his heavy-lidded gaze, screened by his dark glasses, was resting steadily on her...

As if, she thought wildly, he were assessing her...

For what? For my role as his royal bride?

A bead of hysteria formed in her throat, but she suppressed it. Suppressed all her emotions until finally, after a stroll through the manicured grounds, and a short excursion along the river in the hotel's private launch, she and Marika were finally returned to the Viscari St James.

She thanked Leon with what semblance of composure she could muster, only to have him glance a slanting smile at her, his long lashes dipping in a way that brought a flush of colour to her cheek.

'The pleasure was all mine, Princess,' he murmured.

He helped himself to her hand, bowing over it, and Ellie was sure he was doing so to remind her of how he had kissed her hand that night at the opera. There was something about the glint in his eyes that told her so...

Colour ran into her cheeks again and she turned away, glad that her stepmother was making some remark to him. Whatever it was, Ellie caught only his reply.

'Alas, Highness, I am scheduled to be out of the

country for several days on business, but when I return I would be delighted if you would permit me to invite you to dine with me—and the princesses, too, of course.'

He swept a benign smile over Ellie and Marika—who was busying herself with her phone, frantically texting in a way that sank Ellie's heart. The distant beloved, no doubt. Distant and utterly ineligible...

She dragged her mind away from her sister's hopeless predicament, her eyes going to her father and his wife. With their visitor gone, she could see that they were allowing the front they'd put on for him to collapse. Her father looked old and tired—her stepmother tense and strained. They might not say anything to her or Marika, but it was evident that the stress of their precarious situation was eating into them. They knew, even if they did not say it, how grave their predicament was.

If Leon Dukaris pulls the plug on them what will happen to them?

Impossible to imagine—just impossible! A penurious exile? But where? Where would they go? What would they live on?

Fear bit at her, and she could feel it resonating in the room. Could hear, leaping into life yet again, that other question circling in her head.

A princess bride—is that what Leon Dukaris expects for the money he's spending on us? Can he truly be thinking that?

And what if he were? She felt emotion clutch at her. What answer could she possibly give?

What on earth do I tell him if he really, truly wants to marry me?

The only sane answer was no—no, no and *no!* How

could she possibly contemplate even entertaining such
an idea? To marry a stranger…a man she barely knew…

Everything in her revolted. All her life she had
vowed to marry only for love. Hadn't her own parents'
sad example shown how vital that was? Her mother
was very open about how she'd felt so pressured by her
father—flattered that his daughter was being wooed by
a prince, he'd pressed her into a marriage that her royal
husband had wanted only to please *his* own father and
beget an heir to the throne.

It was a marriage that had never worked for either
of them, and they'd parted from each other with relief,
each of them glad to find love and happiness in their
second marriages.

'Never do what I did, darling,' Ellie's mother had
warned her all her life. *'Only marry for love—nothing
else!'*

She felt her emotions twist inside her, tearing her to
pieces, making sleep impossible as she lay tensely staring up at the ceiling in Malcolm's flat that night. For
herself, it would be easy to reject Leon Dukaris's ambitions for a royal bride. As Ellie Peters her own situation was perfectly secure—a home in Somerset with
her mother, a modest salary working for her stepfather's
production company. The freedom to marry for love
and only for love…

But she was more than just her mother's daughter—
more than just Ellie Peters.

*I am also Princess Elizsaveta, daughter of the Grand
Duke of the House of Karpardy, and I have duties and
obligations and responsibilities that are not mine to
evade.*

And the difference was everything.

She took a deep, decisive breath. Resolution filled her. No more endless circling, no more questioning, no more confusion. She must embrace the responsibilities of her royal heritage. Her face tautened. And if that meant setting aside her own personal desires and marrying a man she barely knew—well, so be it.

Decision made, she felt a kind of peace—a feeling of resignation and resolve—come over her. Sleep, long delayed, made her eyelids flutter shut. And as it did, it brought dreams with it—dreams of a strong-featured face, of heavy-lidded, night-dark eyes resting on her. Desiring her… Impatient to make her his bride. His princess bride.

CHAPTER FOUR

Leon watched the princess being ushered to his table across the restaurant and felt the familiar kick go through his system at the sight of her. The days he'd spent away from London had only increased his desire to see her again—and now here she was, walking towards him in all her breathtaking beauty.

She was wearing, he discerned, an outfit by a designer much favoured by the young British royals—a tailored suit in pale green, adorned with very correct pearls, yet again. But there was something about the air with which she carried herself that marked her out as different from just another wealthy young woman.

His expression altered slightly. Except, of course, the Princess Elizsaveta was not a wealthy young woman at all... She was, in fact, penniless. As penniless as the rest of her family.

Unless she marries me.

And she would—he was sure of it. After all, why else inform his PA that she wished to meet him for lunch today?

He got to his feet, murmuring a greeting, and she took her place opposite him. She had an air of calm composure about her, but Leon could sense that she was very far from being either calm or composed. Her every sense was on alert.

As the attentive waiter poured iced mineral water for her, then retreated, Leon sat back, his gaze openly appreciative of her blonde beauty, the soft grey-blue of her eyes, the curve of her mouth, the sculpted line of her high cheekbones, the glorious pale gold of her hair, caught now into a chignon with low-set combs.

He was enjoying the elegance of her poise, the sweet swell of her breasts... She really was so very, very beautiful... He felt his senses stir, warming in his veins. Confirming everything he'd made his decision on. She was, without a shadow of a doubt, the ideal royal bride for him.

She is everything I want—everything!

She was speaking, and he made himself pay attention. She had leant forward slightly, her pose straight-backed, her manner very different from the subdued restraint she adopted when she was with her father and stepmother, or her determinedly polite, impersonal demeanour that afternoon at Meredon. Now her tone of voice was brisk.

'Thank you for agreeing to meet me, Mr Dukaris,' she opened. 'I have, as you may suppose, a particular reason for wanting you to do so.'

Leon veiled his gaze. He said nothing, merely gave a faint smile, waiting for her to continue.

For a moment she seemed unnerved, then she rallied, her tone still brisk. 'I need to be clear,' she went on, her voice deliberately cool, 'about a very important matter.'

* * *

Ellie paused, resting her eyes on his. It was taking her considerable resolve to do so. From the moment she'd set eyes on him across the restaurant, his relaxed but powerful frame had drawn her gaze immediately, and the familiar rush to her blood had sent heat flushing through her. She had had to fight hard to subdue it as she took her place. This was no time for any such reaction to him. She was here for one reason, and one reason only.

'Mr Dukaris, why are you paying for my father's suite at the Viscari St James?'

Leon stilled. He had not anticipated quite so blunt a question. But then, after all, he recollected, she had been just as blunt that night at *Turandot*, when she had, out of nowhere, warned him off her sister.

He heard her continue.

'Since my father now has neither power nor influence in Karylya, you have no obvious need for his favour. So...' she took a breath '...there must be some other reason.'

He saw her lips press together, as if she were steeling herself to go on.

'Tell me,' she said, and her voice was cool, yet Leon could sense the tension in it all the same, 'were you serious, at the opera, in your remark to me? Or was it some clumsy attempt at humour?'

There—she had said it—had finally put into words what had been preying on her mind all week and more. She had finally nerved herself to say what *had* to be said.

A faint smile flickered at his mouth, curving his sensuous lips, but Ellie refused to be distracted by it. She could not afford to be—not now. Far too much depended on his answer.

'It would be humour in a very poor taste, would you not agree?' A slight lift of one dark arched eyebrow accompanied his laconic reply.

'Indeed,' she said tightly. She took a breath, forced herself on. 'And I have to allow that my sister may be quite mistaken in her…her interpretation of just why you are being so generous to my father at this difficult time for him.'

She watched him reach for his glass again, take another leisurely mouthful. He appeared to be infuriatingly relaxed, that long-lashed gaze from his night-dark eyes still veiled, his expression unreadable, yet she could sense there was a sudden tension in him. She held her breath, waiting for his reply on which so much would depend.

Enough to change my life for ever—

The enormity of the moment pressed upon her, and she could hear the slug of her own heartbeat in her chest.

After an age, his answer came. His eyes held hers, still veiled, but it was impossible not to be held by them.

'No, she was not mistaken,' he said. He started to lower his glass to the table. 'Only,' he went on, 'mistaken as to my preference. As I told you, it is not your sister I have an interest in marrying…'

She heard him say it as clear as a bell, and not in any sardonic manner, or with any possible humorous twist, but with a sudden unveiling of his gaze upon her that stilled the breath in her lungs.

'Why?'

The word burst from Ellie—she could not stop it. She realised she had leant forward, giving vehement emphasis to her blunt question.

He paused in the act of lowering his glass. His expression changed minutely.

'Why...?' he echoed.

Then his expression changed again. Ellie could see it—could see his eyes veiling again, a slight smile deliberately forming around that well-shaped mouth of his.

'Why would any man *not* wish to marry a princess?'

The riposte was light, designed to deflect her, she knew. But this was no game, no joke, no humorous light-hearted situation. This was real—brutally, starkly real. Nothing to do with any fairy story...

'Why do *you* want to marry a princess?' Her question was like a scalpel. She wanted an answer and she would have one—a good one, a real one!—or she would walk away from the table right now.

She saw his expression change yet again. She gave a start as she realised that she recognised what she was now seeing in those incredible, long-lashed, gold-glinting night-dark eyes, whose gaze resting on her seemed able to turn her to liquid mush. But they were not doing so now—they were resting on her with something quite different in them. Something she had not seen before but was seeing now.

Honesty.

'I have no idea how much you know about me, Princess,' he said now, his voice as clear-sounding as hers had been, 'but you will have been told, I am sure, that I am nothing more than a jumped-up, *nouveau riche* billionaire who has made a fortune speculating in the global markets. That is quite true, and a moment's search on the Internet will confirm that. There is no secret about that. And nor, by the same token, do I make any secret of the fact that I have more money than I know what to do with.'

He gave the slightest shrug of his shoulder—as if, Ellie thought, all those billions were just toy money.

'I want something else now,' he said.

He set his glass back on the damask tablecloth with a click. Levelled his eyes straight at her.

'I can buy anything I want—anything. But there are some things that are harder to buy. Without help.' He gave a smile now—a tight, knowing smile. 'The help of a princess. A princess as a glittering prize to crown my achievements in life.'

He sat back, his long, strong fingers still curved around his glass, eyes still resting on her with that same startling revelation that what he was doing now was telling her, bluntly and openly, just how it was.

Ellie kept her face still. 'A princess?' she echoed flatly. '*Any* princess?' It was a taunt, a challenge.

That negligent shrug came again. 'More or less,' he admitted. 'Of course the number of available princesses of marriageable age is highly limited, and even those who might be willing to marry someone like me would want to get something for themselves out of it.'

For my family, Ellie told herself. *Only for them.*

Yet even as she thought it she felt a flush go through her. And a thought that was utterly and totally irrelevant to the moment. Any woman who married Leon

Dukaris would be getting *him*—all six-foot-plus of devastating male...

She dragged her thoughts away. They weren't relevant to the brutal discussion she was having...*had* to have...with this man keeping her father from ignominious penury... Who was only doing so in the expectation of a royal bride.

That much was obvious now.

She sat back. She felt as if she was doing a workout with weights too heavy for her. Yet she had to continue. This had to play out to the end.

I have to know exactly what it is I'm letting myself in for. Marrying a man who only wants to marry me for my royal blood—no other reason.

She felt something twist inside her and suppressed it. There was no point in feeling it. No point lamenting that her life-long dream of marrying only for love had become impossible. No point in anything except doggedly continuing.

She took a breath, saying the thing she *had* to say. 'Do you accept, Mr Dukaris, that my sister Marika is *not* "available", as you so charmingly express it?' Ellie could not stop a waspish note stinging her voice. 'Because she is in love with someone else?'

A faintly bored look crossed his face. 'I made that clear the other night, I believe,' he answered. One arched eyebrow lifted. 'With that established, shall we move on?' he invited.

This time the taunt was his, not hers. He was taking control of the agenda, and making it clear to her that he was doing so.

'So, having disposed of the subject of your sister,' his

tone of voice was bland now, 'I assume you are about to set out the terms and conditions of our marriage.'

Leon saw her eyes flash, impartially observing how it lent a dramatic aspect to her pale beauty.

'You take it for granted that I will accept your offer?' she asked.

He gave a shake of his head. 'No, I take it for granted that you do not wish to see your father destitute. And that as a loyal daughter you will do whatever is necessary to prevent that. And, of course…' there was a sardonic note to his voice now '…to enable your sister to remain free to pine after another man.' He frowned for a moment. 'Who *is* she pining for, by the way?'

Ellie's expression changed. 'Someone she'll never be allowed to marry. Antal Horvath.'

Leon's frown deepened. 'Antal Horvath? But isn't that—?'

Ellie's lips pressed together tightly. 'Yes, precisely. Antal is the son of Matyas Horvath—the man who led the coup deposing my father and who aims to be voted President of Karylya in his place!'

Leon's eyebrows rose. 'Well, that unpalatable fact will certainly test her youthful ardour!' he commented sardonically. 'However…' his voice changed '…the woes of your sister are irrelevant to ourselves,' he said dismissively, reaching for the leather-bound menu.

He looked across at the princess he infinitely preferred to her hopelessly lovelorn sister. Satisfaction was rising through him—he was achieving exactly what he wanted, and that always felt good. Very good.

'Shall we get on with ordering lunch?' he invited. He was hungry and he wanted to eat.

He made to flick open the menu, but the princess's voice stayed him.

'Not yet.'

Her tone was commanding, as befitting a princess, and Leon paused, setting down the menu with an air of patience. He lifted an enquiring eyebrow.

Ellie felt her jaw tighten, felt turbid emotions, clashing and turbulent, sloshing inside her. If she really, truly were to do the unthinkable—agree to marry a man she barely knew—she had to be rock-solid sure she would get the protection for her family they needed.

'There are, as you say, terms and conditions.'

She had got her brisk, businesslike tone back, and was relieved she could still adopt it. She took a breath, marshalling her strength to make things crystal-clear to him.

'The first of which is that I want a time limit on this marriage. Two years—no more. That gives you ample time to take all the social advantages you want out of marrying a princess.'

His face was closed. For a second—just a second— Ellie felt a thrill of apprehension go through her. Then, abruptly, his expression changed and he gave a slight assenting shrug of his shoulder, as if the stipulation meant nothing to him.

That stipulation means nothing to me! Of course it doesn't. Why should two years not give me everything I want from her? Why would I care if she leaves me then?

He felt his mind shift away, as if from a place it refused to go. Where it would always refuse to go.

'Good,' Ellie said decisively, relief filling her.

I have to know that I can eventually be free of this marriage—free to find the love I seek.

She forged on, knowing she had to put everything down on the table in one go.

A hefty capital sum settled on her father, yielding an income sufficient to maintain his dignity in exile, and a suitable property for him and his wife to live in *gratis* for their lifetime.

'Oh, and you must guarantee the university fees for my brother Niki—and a dowry for my sister. So that she, at least, will have freedom of choice when it comes to her marriage. Sufficient, if necessary, to defy her parents—' She broke off.

Was there a trace of bitterness in her voice? She hoped not—what was the point of bitterness in the face of brute reality?

Disbelief was possessing her—an air of absolute unreality that she was actually doing what she was doing… marrying a stranger in order to protect her father and his family. To ensure a future for them all.

At the price of mine.

She felt her stomach hollow. That was the truth of it, wasn't it? Everyone got what they wanted except her. She was going to have to hand herself over to a complete stranger, have her own life hijacked by making a marriage to this man she barely knew.

A cry came from deep inside her.

This isn't the marriage I wanted to make! I wanted

*to marry for love—only for love! Even princesses can
marry for love.*

But not this one. Like so many of her ancestors, she
was going to marry for royal duty—because she was
the only one in the family who could protect her father
now, protect her stepmother, her siblings.

She felt a wash of misery flush through her and her
eyes dropped away, her throat tightening.

She heard Leon Dukaris—the vastly rich billionaire
who was going to ensure her family's future at the price
she had agreed to pay for it—agreeing to all she demanded. And for a second—just a second—panic flared
in her eyes. This marriage was going to happen…it really was going to happen! She was going to marry this
man—this complete stranger—whose disturbing gaze
on her could quicken her pulse and confuse her utterly…

The rush of panic beat up inside her again. And then
suddenly she felt her hand being taken. His strong fingers closed around hers. His eyes held her troubled gaze.

Something seemed to run between them. As if, she
thought, for the very first time she was seeing the man
and not the billionaire. Not the devastatingly masculine
male that her feminine senses were continually so perpetually aware of but the person—the individual, with
a character and personality of his own.

A quiver seemed to go through her she could make
no sense of.

'It will be all right, this marriage of ours,' he said
quietly, his eyes still holding hers. 'I will make sure
of it.'

Then, before she could realise his intent, he was lifting her hand to his lips. It was the briefest of hand-

kisses, but as he lowered her hand back to the table and released it Ellie felt, for the very first time since her mother had given her the dreadful news about her father, the agitation inside her and the tumult of her emotions start to subside.

The man she had just agreed to marry smiled. An open, reassuring smile. And somehow—she did not know why or how—all her panic was gone…quite gone.

'Good girl,' she heard Leon Dukaris say approvingly, and he patted the back of her hand.

He looked about, summoning the maître d'.

'Now, let's toast our engagement in champagne! It deserves no less!'

CHAPTER FIVE

ELLIE WAS BUSY. Very busy. Not only was she assembling an extensive couture wardrobe suitable for her role as Leon Dukaris's fiancée and thereafter as his bride, but the wedding itself was to be lavish in the extreme, staggeringly expensive, and, it seemed, with a vast amount for her to do—even with the help of the wedding team at the Viscari.

They were to be married at the hotel, where her family would continue to live until her father and her stepmother and sister moved into a château in the Loire that Leon had purchased for that purpose.

The tabloids and the glossy magazines were in raptures. Ellie might be grimly aware of the real reason for her marriage, but to the world it was a fairy-tale romance.

The Princess and the Greek Tycoon!
Love in Exile!
Royal Bride for Billionaire!

Any number of permutations blazed in the headlines, accompanied by pictures from the carefully staged photo shoots set up by the PR machine activated by Leon Dukaris to show the world he was marrying a princess.

She'd let her father believe the same as the press, for the look of relief in his eyes when she'd told him her news had been painful to behold. If he wanted to keep the comforting illusion that his financial benefactor had taken one look at Elizsaveta and experienced a *coup de foudre* Ellie would not disabuse him.

It was not something she had tried with her mother, however. She and Malcolm were back from Canada, and Ellie had gone down to Somerset to tell her.

It had not been an easy conversation so far. Her mother was protesting strongly, but Ellie defended her decision.

'I can't abandon my father after what's happened to him—'

'Darling—he has *no* right to demand this of you!' her mother began.

But Ellie cut across her. 'He isn't demanding it!' she'd said. 'I'm doing this because I love him—and I want to protect him.'

She took a step back from her mother's anxious embrace, and felt something change in her face. She was no longer Ellie Peters, but Princess Elizsaveta of the Royal House of Karpardy.

'I am my father's daughter,' she said, 'and I have obligations to my birth. It's as simple as that.'

Her mother looked at her, her gaze troubled. 'And what of love?' she said.

Ellie's expression was wry. 'I must hope that I will

be like you and Papa—each of you finding love in a second marriage.'

It was the thought she clung to as the wedding preparations swept her up. Of her fiancé himself she saw not a great deal, and mostly in public or in company. He seemed to be flying about the world a lot, and had told her that he was putting his business affairs in order so that they would not make demands on him after their wedding.

She knew that in a cowardly way she was relieved at his absence. It just seemed easier for her to cope with.

She was relieved, too—though she did not want to spell it out to herself—that when they *were* together he did not take advantage of their engagement to get up close and personal...

Her mind sheered away, blocking such thoughts— she would deal with them later, but not now, she thought hectically. Instead, whenever she was with him, she would take refuge in adopting the same brisk attitude she had at that fateful lunch, when she had committed herself to a man she barely knew.

This time, though, it was endless wedding details that needed agreement—anything and everything, from the music during the ceremony to who the huge guest list should include.

'Both my mother and stepmother are summoning all the relatives they can round up,' she told Leon frankly over dinner, during one of his intermittent stop-overs in London. 'And they're pressing for as many royals— British and European—as we can muster in the time available.'

She ran through a number of the names of people who had RSVP'd already.

'Very impressive,' acknowledged Leon dryly.

Had that been a sardonic note in his voice? Ellie lifted her chin.

'Well, that's what this is all about, isn't it?' she riposted, in the same openly frank manner. 'Making as big a social splash with our wedding and our marriage as we can?'

Leon sat back in his chair—they were at the same restaurant they had been for lunch all those weeks ago, when she had sealed her fate. Perhaps that was why she was speaking so frankly now, making herself face the reason she was marrying Leon Dukaris. To give him a princess bride to crown his achievements and give her beleaguered father the financial security he so desperately needed.

And it's for no other reason—none.

Leon had made that clear—he had spoken no soft, seductive words to the contrary, cast no lingering glances at her, made no pretence that he felt anything for her. So, however much she might find her heart rate starting to quicken when she was with him, however heavy-lidded that dark, gold-flecked gaze of his could be, resting on her with that veiled expression she could not make out, she had to set all that aside.

His expression now, though, was not veiled at all. His eyes had narrowed as she'd spoken.

'Tell me,' he said, and there was a silky note to his voice that she had not heard before, for usually he gave quick, good-humoured answers to her questions, 'do you intend always to be this blunt about our marriage?'

Ellie felt colour flush her cheeks, but fought it back. Lifted her chin again. Met that narrowed gaze full-on. Th world might be cooing over them, lavishing them with a romantic gloss that sold magazines by the truckload, but she would not collude with it. She would not pretend there was anything between them but what there was.

There was a spark in her eyes as she answered him. 'Leon, you're marrying me because I'm a princess, and I'm marrying you because you're rich enough to bankroll my father and his family. My title for your wealth. It's a pretty blunt situation,' she said unrepentantly.

She held his gaze, which all of a sudden was like coruscating black diamonds. She reeled from the impact of it—but she would not flinch. Then, abruptly, that coruscating gaze was gone—veiled by the long dark lashes sweeping down over those gold-flecked eyes. She saw him lift his wineglass and tilt it lazily towards her. The sudden tension in him relaxed. He smiled his familiar half-sardonic, half-open smile.

'Well, then, let us drink to our marriage all the same,' said Leon equably. 'An honest marriage…'

As most marriages are not—with the couple deluding each other with the belief that eternal love will bind them, when the first misfortune to befall them will make a mockery of all their vows!

So why should he care if his beautiful royal bride was being so blunt about why they were marrying? It was only the truth.

Except that it is not the only *truth… It is not simply*

because I want a princess bride to show off on my arm and she wants a dignified exile for her father.

There was another truth to their marriage. As potent a truth as those.

He veiled his expression as she touched her glass to his with a faint answering smile, concealing his thoughts, knowing that she was not yet ready for anything more from him.

But perhaps it's time...

Perhaps it was time that Princess Elizsaveta realised that he was marrying her for a great deal more than her title...

As he took another ruminative sip of his wine, watching with pleasure the way her delicate features caught the soft light pooling over their table as she skimmed her gaze over the next item on the wedding list, he knew exactly the occasion for her to do so.

The glittering opulence of their betrothal ball.

It would be ideal...

Ellie took a steadying breath, gathering her skirts. There were a lot of them—a cloud of palest blush-pink organza and chiffon—and her boned bodice was encrusted with crystal, another billowing swathe of chiffon framing her bare shoulders and arms. At her throat an ornate pink diamond necklace matched the long drop earrings of the parure, as did the twin bracelets encircling her wrists and the combs holding her elaborate upswept hair.

The very image of a princess.

At least I'm not wearing a coronet! she thought wryly to herself.

She'd drawn the line at that, explaining to Leon that tiaras were only worn by married women—indeed, her mother, sitting beside her in the huge limo now drawing up at the Viscari, was so doing.

'Heaven knows when I last wore this!' her mother had exclaimed when her jewellery case had arrived from its safety deposit box at her bank.

Her voice had been light, but her expression troubled. And Ellie knew why—tonight would be the first time her mother would meet Leon, the man who was bailing out her ex-husband at the price of her daughter's hand in marriage.

'I won't say a word, darling, I promise you—this is your choice and you have made it in good conscience. I will stand by you,' her mother had said, and Ellie had been deeply grateful. Grateful, too, to have her mother and stepfather with her tonight.

The doorman was stepping forward, opening the limo door, and with a final intake of breath Ellie got out, taking the greatest care with her voluminous ball gown. As she did she heard a scatter of applause from the gathered onlookers, saw the flash of cameras, and realised that Leon's PR machine was ensuring that a quiet entrance was going to be impossible.

Then her mother and stepfather were beside her and they were all walking into the hotel. And in the marble-floored, mahogany-furnished atrium Leon was crossing the space towards them.

As it always did, Ellie felt her breath catch. Of all the men in the world, in evening dress Leon Dukaris beat them hands-down. He just looked...*superb*! And in white tie—for this was a fully formal evening—the effect was tripled.

'Princess…'

He was taking her hand, bowing over it but not kissing it. His eyes were fastened on her, and in them was an expression that was like a blaze.

'You look *incredible*!' he breathed.

His gaze washed over her, taking in every detail of her sumptuous attire. She wanted to say something—anything! To make some light-hearted remark—something about Cinderella arriving for the ball, maybe, or something about a fairy-tale—whatever she could think of to say with a smile.

But she couldn't. She couldn't say a word as his blazing eyes devoured her. The breath had gone from her lungs, her head had emptied of anything at all except his gaze feasting upon her.

And then, dimly, she became aware that her mother and stepfather were waiting to be introduced to the man she was going to marry.

She had to make a huge effort but she drew back her hand, wishing it weren't quivering like a leaf in autumn. 'Leon, may I present you to my mother?' she murmured, trying to stop her voice quivering helplessly.

As if he were also coming to himself, Leon's expression changed, becoming formal. He turned towards her mother. 'Lady Constance,' he said, 'I'm delighted to meet you at last,' he said.

'And I you, Mr Dukaris,' Ellie heard her mother reply, with an assessing note in her voice.

'Leon, please…' he replied immediately.

'Then you had better call me Connie,' she invited.

There seemed, Ellie thought, to be a warmer note in her mother's voice now, and wondered at it, but was grateful, too.

'Lady Connie,' Leon compromised, his smile coming again as he turned to Ellie's stepfather.

Ellie performed the requisite introduction, and was glad that Leon's demeanour acknowledged that her stepfather was a man of some renown in his field.

As Leon made graceful reference to his work, and Malcolm made a jovial reply in his usual bluff and forthright manner, Ellie glanced around her. She frowned. The only people in the huge Edwardian-style atrium apart from some senior hotel staff were, she realised from their black-suited, discreetly tough-looking appearance, Security.

Leon had clearly seen her glance at them, and he took her arm and ushered them all towards the grand staircase sweeping up to the first-floor ballroom.

'The hotel is in lockdown until we are in the ballroom,' he said. 'Just a precaution, given both your family and the people on the guest list.'

Ellie just nodded. It wasn't just a precaution—she knew that. But she did not say so, for what would be the point? It was so the world could see and know that Leon Dukaris was marrying royalty, and that royalty were not like other mere mortals on this earth.

It was why, too, he went on addressing her mother as Lady Connie—highlighting that even on her mother's side, there was ancient nobility—albeit not royal. Her uncle, the Earl of Holmsworth, would be at the wedding, and his two young daughters were to be her flower girls, his ten-year-old son her page boy.

But before the wedding there was tonight's ball to get through.

Leaning on Leon's arm slightly more heavily than she'd thought she would need to, because of the sudden weakness in her limbs caused by his presence at her side, she processed with him up the sweeping staircase, then entered the vast, ornate ballroom, festooned with flowers and ablaze with light from a dozen crystal chandeliers, to receive another smattering of applause from the assembled guests.

Ellie smiled about her, but Leon was heading towards the far end, where her father and stepmother were. Two large gilded chairs had been procured, and the Grand Duke and Duchess were presiding over the whole affair.

Dutifully, Ellie curtsied when she reached them, her skirts billowing out in a cloud of blush-pink. Her father, splendid in white tie and tails, stood up and came forward to kiss her, then shook Leon's hand as he bowed. Behind him the Grand Duchess dipped her head in regal acknowledgement of their arrival, and beside her Marika—looking enchantingly pretty in pale blue—gave her a little wave.

The Grand Duke held up his hand, then announced to the assembled company that he was welcoming them all to the betrothal ball of his daughter and her chosen husband-to-be.

'The first dance is theirs!' he declared, and resumed his seat as the orchestra, placed on a raised platform to one side of the room, struck up.

It was a Strauss waltz, and with a strange little catch in her throat, finding it impossible to resist such familiar and lilting music, Ellie went into Leon's arms. She raised her left hand to his shoulder, had her right clasped in his firm grip. For a moment, as his arm came about her waist and he drew her closer to him, she felt her legs weaken further, felt heady at his closeness, and then, as the music sounded, he whirled her across the polished floor.

She gave a little gasp, her eyes darting to his. She held his gaze, unable to break the hold of it—for it was the fulcrum around which she was turning, around which the whole world seemed to be turning. Everything was becoming a blur but not the deep, dark eyes holding hers. And in them—not in their depths, but at the blazing forefront of his gaze—was molten gold. Pure molten gold...

And she melted into it. Just melted...

Suddenly, out of nowhere, the significance of the evening became clear—here she was, in this utterly over-the-top concoction of a ball gown, bedecked with jewellery, her satin slippers twirling her body around, caught in the arms of this impossibly devastating man, whose dark looks and planed face and sable hair were so ludicrously flattered by the white tie and tails that moulded his powerful body like a glove.

It's like a fairy-tale! A fairy-tale of mythical princesses and handsome heroes!

But it wasn't a fairy-tale!

It was true—all of it!

She was waltzing to the music of Strauss, the Waltz King, and she was Princess Elizsaveta of Karylya, and Leon Dukaris was— Oh, he was the most handsome man who had ever walked the earth!

She was enchanted, beguiled and enthralled, spinning around and around to music that no soul on earth could resist, to the music that whirled in her blood, carrying her slippered feet across the ballroom…

And she could not take her eyes from Leon. Not for anything in heaven and earth. Not while the music played, and she danced and she danced in his arms…

With a crescendo of sound, the music stopped. The waltz was over and she was standing there, heart pounding, the blood singing in her veins, exhilaration, wonder and enchantment consuming her.

She was still gazing up at Leon, and he was still holding her in his dancer's hold, his hand at her waist. Then she felt her hand released, and hers fell to her side, nerveless with exhaustion. She could feel her heart beating so strongly—with the exertion of the dance, and with so much more than that.

She drank him in—the chiselled planes of his face, the sculpted mouth, the dark, drowning gaze of his eyes holding hers. She felt his other hand slip from her waist and she swayed, as if he alone had been holding her steady. And then, with a catch in her throat, she felt him cup her face with his long, strong fingers, tilting it up towards him, the touch of his hands catching at her breath. Her lips parted…helpless, breathless…

'My Princess…'

His voice was low, and warm, and for her and her alone. And his lips, when they touched hers, were warm and for her and her alone. And his kiss was warm and slow and for her and her alone.

She felt her eyes flutter shut, felt the soft, sensuous glide of his mouth on hers, felt a liquefying rush go through her as if every cell in her body was dissolving. It seemed to go on and on, that kiss…on and on and on…

When his mouth lifted from hers she could only stare, dazed, helpless, her lips still parted. She kept on gazing up at him as his hands slid from her face and he smiled down at her.

'My Princess…' he said again, his voice husky.

Then he was tucking her limp hand that suddenly seemed to weigh half a ton into the crook of his arm and he was leading her off the dance floor. And she had to lean into him because she had no strength left in her body…not the slightest bit of strength.

Her mind was a daze, her thoughts a whirl, and the orchestra was striking up again. She was aware that other couples were taking to the floor now, and that Leon was leading her back to where her family sat, her mother and stepfather beside the royal couple, though on less ornate chairs. Marika was being led out onto the dance floor by someone Ellie vaguely recognised as one of the junior members of the British royal family, and seemingly very happy.

But she had no thoughts to spare for her sister or her parents, or for the throng of glittering guests here tonight to see Leon Dukaris present his royal bride-to-be to the world. She had no thoughts at all for anyone at all who was not the man who had swept her onto the dance floor and kissed her like the Princess in a fairy-tale…

Who had taken her, with that waltz and that kiss, to an enchanted realm she never wanted to leave…

CHAPTER SIX

LEON STOOD UNDER the rose-decked silk canopy as the celebrant threw him an encouraging smile. Yet for all that he could feel tension netting him. This was the day, the moment, when he would marry. Would marry his princess bride.

From that original fancy over a year ago, when the idea of marrying a princess had first come to him, to this moment now, when it was actually about to happen, seemed a blur.

Was he mad to do this? To truly go ahead with it?

Marriage was not an affair—it was unknown territory...

Unease flickered in his consciousness. Even with all the safeguards he had placed around what he was doing, ensuring that no delusions of love could come anywhere near this marriage, and that he and the woman he was to wed were doing so for reasons that had nothing to do with any such illusory notions, still unease flickered within him.

Memories, toxic and cruel, plucked at his mind.

Almost he gave them admittance.

Then, with a sudden rustle of movement amongst

the serried ranks of guests behind him, he heard the music, up to this moment low and forgettable, start to swell, switching into full volume to herald the arrival of his bride.

He turned.

He could not stop himself.

And as his eyes lit upon her all doubts fled...

Ellie took a breath, pressed her hand on her father's arm. The music was swelling—the Royal Anthem of Karylya, insisted on by her father. And who was she to deny him this small comfort, when he did not even have his royal regalia any longer, and had to walk his daughter down the aisle in nothing more than commonplace morning dress.

The guests were getting to their feet with a scraping of chairs on the paved ground of the Viscari roof terrace. The unreliable English weather was blessedly clement, so that recourse to the glass conservatory along one side of the rooftop would be unnecessary—except for the serving of the wedding breakfast to follow.

An arbour of roses arched across the aisle and their scent caught at her, adding to the scent from the thousands more blooms arranged to beautify the already stunning landscape architecture of this green oasis high above the city, enclosed and private, far above the masses on the streets below, where the London traffic was quite inaudible.

She could see the celebrant, waiting for them at the far end of the aisle. A civil ceremony was what she had stipulated to Leon—yet even so she still felt a hypocrite as she stepped towards the man waiting to marry her.

The words she'd so bluntly put to Leon echoed in her head.

'Leon, you're marrying me for my title, and I'm marrying you because you're rich enough to bankroll my father and his family.'

Everything—all this extravaganza of a wedding, the guest list crammed with aristocrats and royalty, leaked to the press and the media by Leon for maximum coverage—was for that reason alone.

Yet even though she knew it she felt again the magical brush of Leon's lips on hers, the enchantment of his kiss whispering of reasons that had nothing to do with her father's exile, her bridegroom's ambitions... reasons that fluttered like a butterfly seeking the sweetest nectar...

She felt her hand tremble on her father's arm, and he patted it reassuringly as they processed forward. Nerves plucked at her, but she knew she must not let them show. Must be as composed, as calm, as perfect a princess bride as she could be.

Do her family proud.

Do Leon proud by being the perfect princess bride for him.

Beneath her veil her eyes went to him, and she was glad of the veil to hide the sudden heating of her cheeks. An air of unreality pressed upon her, as if she could not believe this was truly happening. But all her training came to the fore—as it must.

They reached the celebrant, the anthem ended and the congregation resumed their seats. Leon stepped forward to stand beside her. Her father stepped back to join his wife. Her mother and stepfather flanked them.

Behind her Marika, her bridesmaid, took her allotted place, ushering the little flower girls to theirs, their older brother bringing up the rear.

The celebrant began to speak...

She heard the words but did not hear them. Heard her own voice but did not hear it. Heard Leon's but did not hear it. Let Leon take her hand, slide the wedding band on her nerveless finger, his touch cool. She said more words, and so did he, and then the celebrant was speaking again, to them both.

Joining them in matrimony.

And she was Leon's princess bride.

'Where are we going?' Ellie asked her new husband with mild enquiry.

Leon moved into the London traffic, shifting gear in the million-pound, brand-new supercar delivered that very morning—an enjoyable present to himself for his wedding day.

'Wait and see,' he answered.

He had told her nothing about his plans for a honeymoon, and wanted it to be a surprise. A pleasing one, he hoped...

They had been waved off amidst laughter and an easily foiled attempt by his new bride's brother—finished now with his schooldays—and some of the younger males among the wedding guests to attach rattling tin cans to the bumper. Instead they had contented themselves by spraying 'Just married!' in shaving foam on the gleaming rear end of the car.

His bride's flower girls—Ellie's cousins Lady Emily and Lady Rose—had excitedly festooned them, and the car bonnet, with flower blossoms, giggling madly as their brother, the young Viscount, had vigorously popped streamers into the car's interior.

Leon had tolerated it all with smiling equanimity. These harmless aristocratic antics were, after all, what he was paying for. Just as he was paying for his bride's father and his family to enjoy their exile in luxury at his expense.

And in exchange…

His eyes slid to his bride. No longer in her wedding finery, she had changed into an ivory silk couture number and five-inch heels—which, Leon noticed with wry amusement, she was now kicking off into the spacious footwell with a sigh of relief.

'That bad?' he said sympathetically, nodding at the discarded killer heels.

'Not my thing,' she answered feelingly.

'You looked fabulous in them, though,' Leon said, as he headed down Piccadilly towards Hyde Park Corner.

'Well, that was the idea,' Ellie answered easily.

The shoes were part of her brand-new couture wardrobe, wearing which she would grace the arm of her billionaire husband when he showed off his princess bride to the world. Already engagements had been set, and they had a crammed social diary that would take them to one upper-crust event after another across Europe and beyond. They would be doing the Season—*all* the Seasons—and being seen at the best places with the best people, a high-flying, jet-setting couple who combined royalty and riches in a dazzling display.

It wouldn't be the life Ellie was used to. As Ellie Peters her only international travel was to jungle and tundra with Malcolm and her mother. Even as Princess Elizsaveta of Karylya she had usually stayed only in her homeland, accompanying her stepmother and sister to whatever royal functions they were involved with.

But if her husband wanted them to jet around the world in a glittering swirl of royalty and aristocracy, then that was what they would do. It was what she had signed up to.

Was that what he was intending for their honeymoon? Some ultra-fashionable luxury location half the world away? she wondered as they headed out of London.

But when Leon told her the drive would be a couple of hours, Ellie started to relax. The day had been long, with an early start for all the preparations needed to turn her into a royal bride in all her finery, and the lavish wedding breakfast had seemed to go on for ever. Now, in the late afternoon, she felt tiredness wash over her, and the smooth motion of the powerful car began to cradle her into drowsiness...

At her side, Leon watched her translucent eyelids flutter shut, her breathing slow.

He let her sleep.

Who knew how long the night ahead would be? And all the nights to come thereafter...

Pleasurable anticipation started to fill him. At last this most breathtakingly beautiful woman was his—and their honeymoon awaited...

* * *

Ellie stirred, blinking. 'Where are we?' she asked, looking around. Then, as she took in her surroundings, she gave a little gasp of pleasure.

Beyond the small gravelled parking area the reed-edged waters of a lake beckoned, girdled by broad-leaved forest all around. It was totally private, totally remote.

Leon cut the engine, turning to her. 'Do you like it?' He smiled.

'Oh, *yes*!'

She was slipping her shoes on, opening her car door and stepping out, and Leon did likewise.

Satisfaction was filling him—her reaction was just what he wanted.

He led the way forward, through screening willows and alders, to gain the wooden boardwalk edging the lake that glittered darkly in the late sunshine. The only sign of habitation was a cottage set a little further on.

'It's like a gingerbread house!' Ellie exclaimed pleasurably as she spotted it.

A manservant was emerging from the cottage, and Leon exchanged a few words with him. He would fetch their luggage and then leave them entirely in peace unless summoned.

Inside the cottage, tea had been set out in a comfortably appointed sitting room, whose wide bi-fold doors opened directly on to a broad deck flooded with sunshine.

Ellie turned to him. 'Oh, Leon, this is absolutely *lovely*!' She smiled warmly, her eyes lighting up. 'Ah, tea!' she exclaimed gratefully, sinking down on one of the two sofas, easing her feet out of her killer shoes again before reaching for the teapot and pouring for them both.

'So, what do you think of it?' Leon asked, taking the cup she held out for him.

'It's delightful!' she said warmly. 'And quite a surprise. I thought—' She broke off, stirring milk into her tea.

'Yes?'

Leon's prompt was pointed. She made a slight face and looked up at him.

'Well, I thought you would want somewhere more… public. Glitzy. You know, to—' She broke off again.

An eyebrow rose quizzically. 'To show you off? My royal bride?'

Was there an edge in his voice? He hadn't intended it, but perhaps it was there all the same.

She was looking straight at him now. 'Well, yes,' she answered frankly. 'After all, there's no point marrying a princess and then hiding her away, is there?' She spoke lightly, as if determined not to make too big a deal of it but not to shirk from it either.

He sat back, crossing one long over the other. 'I'm not sure that I want to share you with anyone right now,' he murmured, and he let his eyelids half close as his eyes rested on her. 'I think I want you all to myself…'

He saw a gratifying flush of colour stain her cheeks—only a swift wash, but it was revealing, and that was what he wanted.

He gave a laugh, to lighten the moment. 'And anyway, we've been on show the whole day—I think we deserve some relaxing time "offstage", don't you?

And...' his eyes went to the deck beyond the open bi-folds '...this certainly seems to fit the bill for that!'

'Oh, it *does*!' The warmth was back in her voice. 'I'm so looking forward to exploring! Can we do that?'

'We can do anything we want,' Leon returned. 'It's our honeymoon, and we get to choose.'

He saw her eyes flicker again and knew why. It was the H word that had done it.

Because ours is not the kind of honeymoon an ordinary couple would be having...

But a honeymoon it was, for all that. And it would bring all the pleasures every honeymoon should bring...

He would ensure it.

Ellie sat at the old-fashioned, chintz-skirted, kidney-shaped dressing table in her bedroom and stared at her reflection. The gingerbread cottage was far too homely for a couture outfit, so she'd donned one of her own well-worn favourites—a mauve knee-length dress in fine jersey, with a boat neck and three-quarter sleeves. She fastened her hair with a simple barrette, then slipped her feet into comfortable low-heeled sandals and headed downstairs.

Her mood was strange—uncertain. Up to this point all her energies—mental and physical—had been focussed exclusively on making her wedding happen. And now it had. And she was here with Leon.

Alone with Leon—

She felt her heart rate start to skip, conscious of her quickening pulse and an air of nervousness as she headed down the narrow flight of stairs to the small sitting room. She thought there was something she ought to be thinking about—that she ought to have thought about for quite some time, but she had been too swept up in all the wedding preparations.

She felt it hovering at the back of her mind...knew it was time to bring it to the forefront. Face the implications of it...

But not right now. Her mind skittered away from it, not wanting to confront it.

I'll think about it later.

For now she would simply deal with the evening immediately ahead.

Leon's words to her over tea floated across her mind.

'I think we deserve some relaxing time...'

It was a sentiment that appealed.

In the sitting room, Leon was already there. A table-lamp had been lit against the night gathering outside, giving it a cosy feel. He turned from the drinks trolley, and as his eyes fell on her Ellie felt again that quickening of her pulse, that consciousness of his looks and masculinity that she always felt.

'An aperitif before dinner?' he asked pleasantly.

'Please,' she answered, opting for a sweet martini.

As she took it from him she thought she saw his gaze flicker over her, and was suddenly conscious that perhaps the jersey dress was just a little too softly draped over her body. But then her eyes flickered to him in turn, and she was conscious of how comfortably informal Leon was looking, too, with an open-necked shirt, turned back cuffs and a cashmere sweater slung casually over his shoulders. He looked, as ever, effortlessly drop-dead gorgeous...

'It's a mild evening—shall we go out on the deck?' Leon suggested.

She smiled and let him usher her out. Night was gathering over the lake, and there was the low sound of water lapping beneath the decking and an owl calling from nearby in the woods, then another from further away. She wandered across to the wooden balustrade at the edge of the deck, leaning on it to look over the lake.

'A pair of tawnies,' Ellie announced. Then, listening again, 'And a barn owl, too!'

'How can you tell?' Leon asked, coming up beside her.

She was glad to tell him, for it was a safely innocuous subject, and would help to take her mind off the fact that Leon was standing right beside her, his sleeve brushing hers from time to time as he sipped at his own gin-based cocktail in a leisurely fashion.

She launched into a description of the different kinds of owl hooting, giving a good impression of each herself that made him laugh, and her as well. Their shared laughter made her feel more comfortable... companionable.

'How do you know all that?' he asked with a smile.

'I grew up with a naturalist, remember?' she replied. 'Malcolm was a wonderful teacher.'

There was a fond note in her voice and Leon did not miss it.

'You've been fortunate in your stepfather,' he heard himself say.

'*And* my father.' Her rejoinder was adamant. 'I may only have spent school holidays with him, but they were always happy times. He loves me dearly. And I him. It's why I—'

She broke off, but Leon could hear the unspoken ending of her declaration.

It's why I married you.

He shifted his stance, wanting to change the topic. Away from why she had married him. Away from fathers altogether.

His thoughts twisted inside him. His own father had thought of no one but himself, putting himself first, his own interests, and if that meant deserting the wife he'd professed to love, and their son, too, well, he'd done it without a second thought. Abandoned them to their fate. Thinking nothing of them.

And is her father any better? Happy to see his own daughter married off to a complete stranger just so he can have a luxurious exile?

He felt a flicker of contempt go through him, familiar to him from the contempt he'd always felt for his own father. He, too, had once believed his father loved him—loved the wife he'd kept telling how much he adored her. Until he'd walked out on her.

So much for love...

He would have none of it.

His eyes went to his bride. Well, love had nothing to do with *their* marriage, and he didn't want it to. They'd gone into it clear-eyed, the pair of them, for mutual advantage, and each was getting something out of it that they wanted. That was enough.

He veiled his eyes suddenly. And, of course, for one

other essential reason. The reason he'd brought his bride here to this remote, secluded spot…entirely private.

To claim her as my bride—in every way.

CHAPTER SEVEN

WITH A GESTURE of reluctant refusal Ellie pushed back the plate of exquisite hand-made liqueur chocolate truffles Leon was proffering.

'I couldn't eat even one more!' She gave a mock groan.

'We'll save the rest for tomorrow.' Leon smiled.

Dinner had been provided by staff who'd arrived at the cottage and then left again once the main course had been served. Ellie had made the kind of anodyne conversation with Leon that strangers could overhear, but once they'd gone she'd become conscious of a different kind of constraint—that of being with Leon on her own.

She was grateful, therefore, that he had continued with the same mild and genial air he'd adopted since they'd left their wedding, telling her about the cottage and its original Victorian owner, of his enthusiasm for wildfowl. That had led to wildlife in general, and then they had moved on to her stepfather's work, with Leon drawing her out about her experiences travelling with him and her mother on filming expeditions.

Ellie had felt herself relaxing more, regaling him with anecdotes about her adventurous travels in remote locations, where physical comforts had been scarce, and that had taken them through the rest of the meal.

Now, after pushing away the plate of truffles, she finished a particularly hair-raising account of privation and Leon frowned.

'Your mother couldn't have a more different lifestyle now than the one she had with your father—a royal palace versus roughing it in the middle of nowhere!'

Ellie laughed. 'She never could stand all the palace protocol and ceremony! It was bad enough being the Crown Princess, but being Grand Duchess never suited her—it was good that she found the courage to leave a marriage she felt she'd been pressured into by her parents' ambitions for her. They were dazzled by her royal suitor. It never worked for either of them. She's so much happier with Malcolm. And I know my father is so happier with my stepmother. My parents were right to part. No one should stay in an unhappy marriage.'

She saw Leon's face tighten. Had it been tactless to talk about marriages ending when theirs had only just begun? However unlike a normal marriage theirs was?

But his words dispelled any noting that he'd been thinking about their own marriage.

'But what if the wish to part isn't mutual?' he said. 'If it suits only one of the parties?'

There was a harshness in his voice that made Ellie speak carefully. 'That's…difficult,' she allowed.

'Difficult…?' he echoed, as if the word were a derisory understatement.

She looked at him, concern in her eyes. 'That sounds personal,' she said carefully.

Dark eyes flashed across the table at her. His words

were stark when he spoke. 'My father walked out on my mother at the height of the economic collapse in Greece. We'd gone from affluence to poverty. He was a well-paid civil servant, suddenly sacked when the government ran out of money to pay him. He didn't like it—and so he took off with another woman who had money stashed abroad. Left my mother and me to fend for ourselves.'

'Oh, Leon, I'm so sorry!'

Instinctively she reached her hand out to his, but he'd seized up his cognac glass and taken a heavy mouthful, as if he needed it. As he set it down she saw his features lighten again, as if he were making a deliberate effort. Blanking the past.

He pushed back his chair, getting to his feet. 'Shall we get some fresh air?' she heard him ask, and his tone of voice was deliberately lighter.

It was understandable that he wanted to change the subject, for who would want to dwell on such painful memories? So Ellie followed him out on to the deck, to lean, like him, against the wooden railing, gazing out over the dark surface of the lake.

The country air was fresh, and sweet, after so many weeks in London, and she gave a sigh of pleasure. She felt a wash of sympathy for him—for his blighted youth, his plunge into sudden poverty, his father's desertion.

How little I know about him—about the man he is.

But then, how could she know more? Theirs was an artificial marriage—they were still strangers essentially.

Yet as he glanced down at her now there was a familiarity about the way he was smiling at her. A growing sense of ease between them.

'It's good, isn't it, this place?' Leon said, indicating with a nod the quiet, dim vista around them.

The night was cloudy, with a faint mild breeze ruffling the waters of the lake quietly lapping below the deck. Another owl hooted softly, adding to the peaceful atmosphere.

'Yes,' she said, nodding in slow agreement, 'it's good.'

She looked up at him. Returned his smile. But as she did so she saw, even in the low light, his expression change. Become…*searching*. And as it changed she felt something change within herself, felt a sudden consciousness of the two of them, standing out here, all on their own, far from anywhere and anyone else, with the whole world, or so it seemed, to themselves.

It seemed a very private moment. Very…intimate.

She felt her breath tighten in her lungs, wanted to look away, suddenly supremely conscious of his presence at her side. A tendril of hair fluttered at her cheek in the faint breeze, the air soft on her face. Her senses seemed heightened, the pulse at her throat tangible. Out of nowhere came the memory of that first waltz at their betrothal ball…of the kiss that had ended it. She felt the memory bring its sweetness again…

At the back of her mind she felt the thought she did not wish to think stir once more, seeking admittance. She held it back, held it at bay. Instead she gave herself to what she wanted to do, what she always wanted to do…what she had wanted to do from the very first.

She gazed up at his face, drinking him in, watching

those dark, heavy-lidded eyes that were looking down at her in return, half veiled by those long, inky lashes.

Once before he had looked into her eyes like that... As the music of the waltz had ended and his hands had cupped her face, tilting it to his...

They did it again now.

His touch was cool as he cradled her cheeks, his fingertips drifting over the delicate lobes of her ears, teasing at the wafting tendrils of her hair. His face bent to hers, lips catching hers. She felt weakness drum through her...felt her eyelids flutter shut. Felt his mouth—his skilled, silken mouth—move on hers slowly, softly, sensuously.

She opened her mouth to his...

She felt her pulse surge, her lips part under his, her pliant body leaning into him as if her body were taking control of her, yielding to its own impulses, its own needs, its own demands. As his kiss deepened she felt the arousal of her quickened senses, her hands slipping to his chest, feeling the strong, hard wall of muscle beneath her splaying fingers.

Her body quickened, blood surging in her veins, and a flame caught fire within her that was not of her conscious being. It came from a place far, far deeper inside her—a hunger that had come from nowhere, possessing her...

Her mouth clung to his and a low moan broke from her throat. The sense of being possessed by more than she was seared within her. Her kiss deepened, feeding the hunger that had leapt within her. A hunger for him... for Leon...for his mouth, his body...

And it was a hunger he shared, for now his hands

were sliding down to her shoulders, around her waist, fastening over her hips, moving lower still…

The hunger leapt inside her again, possessing her, and she felt her breasts engorge and flower. Another low moan broke from her throat and her body pressed itself against his, seeking more…so much more…

There was nothing else in all the world except this… now…and nothing mattered except this…now…as their mouths moved together, seeking, finding…

With a sudden rasping breath he hauled her close against him, his kisses devouring her. They were hip to hip, their bodies melding together, moulding together…

And his body was reacting to that closeness.

With a shocked gasp she pulled away, rearing back from him even though his hands still anchored her at her hips. She stared at him, eyes distended, lips still bee-stung from his. Her heart was pounding. Dear God, what had she done? To go from that soft, sensuous kiss to…to…

Her mind sheered away and her body did, too. Now she was pulling herself free from him, clutching at the wooden railings, head bowed, fighting for composure…

'What is it? What's wrong?'

Leon spoke behind her, concern in his voice—and alarm. She could hear his breathing, heavier than it had been during conversation, and knew hers was just as hectic. Her heart was still hammering as if she'd run a race. As if she'd been swept away on a flood tide that she had never before experienced. Had never before known the power of.

But she knew it now.

'Tell me! Tell me what is wrong!'

Leon's voice came again, still filled with concern and alarm.

'Leon— I…' She tried to speak, but could not. Tried to look at him, but could not.

Her head dropped again, shoulders hunched. Heat flushing through her. And dismay. Dismay that she had allowed what she should never have allowed to overwhelm her as it had!

Her grip on the railings spasmed.

I should have faced it sooner—not hidden it away, out of sight, while I was burying myself in all those wedding preparations, blanking it. And now…

She started. Leon's large, square hand had lowered over hers, lifting her fingers free of the rail. Gently but inexorably. She felt his presence behind her. He was turning her now, towards him, leading her away from the balustrade, lowering her down upon a wide rattan settee on legs that were suddenly too weak to hold her. Sitting down beside her.

'Tell me,' he said quietly. He did not let go of her hand. 'Tell me what's wrong.'

Her eyes flew to his. Then dropped away again. And still she could not speak. Her skin was burning…her lungs were bereft of air.

'Elizsaveta, look at me.'

Uncertainly, she lifted her eyes to him as he spoke again. His voice was quiet still, but filled with an intensity that accentuated his slight accent.

'Have I confused you?' he asked.

His gaze was searching hers in the dim light. Only the lamplight from the sitting room behind them spilled out onto the deck.

A faint smile tugged at his mouth, and there was a rueful tone in his voice as he spoke again. 'I have been a very…inattentive fiancé, I know—but there was a purpose to it. Yes, I had to settle my business affairs—but there was another reason, too. I could not trust myself to be with you too much. Do you not know why that was?'

He paused, and now his gaze on her was not rueful, nor the tone of his voice.

'Did you really think I was marrying you only for your royal blood?' he was saying now, in that same quiet voice, with the warmth of his hand over hers, stilling the trembling of her limbs. 'Did you really think there was no other reason?' And now there was something else in his voice—an edge, and yet it was an edge softened by wryness.

He paused, and she could feel his thumb brush across the back of her hand with a slow, sensuous touch that seemed to be both calming her and soothing her jangled nerves.

His eyes held hers, their expression changing, and in the stricken veins of her body she felt her pulse quicken…like a ghost of what it had been before she'd torn herself away from him.

'Did I not show you with every look I gave you?' His voice was husky, his eyes fixed on hers. 'Show you when I kissed you at our betrothal ball…?'

She felt colour flush into her cheeks and knew he could see it, even in this dim light.

He was speaking again, in the same husky voice, and the slow brush of his thumb on her hand was still soft and sensuous. 'And when I kissed you then do you think I could not tell how you felt about me in return?

And when I kissed you just now do you think I could not tell how the same flame you light in me every time you look at me, caught fire in you as well?' The husk in his voice was yet more pronounced. 'And do you think,' he finished, 'I would have married you if I did not desire you—if I did not know that same flame burned in both of us?'

He paused, giving a wry half-smile that tugged at his mouth. She gazed at him, wishing with all her being that she had not tried to shut out what had been in her head all along, what she had pushed down and back and out of sight and thought. Now it was here—standing foursquare between them.

Leon was speaking again, still with that quiet, reassuring warmth in his voice, yet there was an underlying timbre to it that plucked at her senses.

'We are married, yes, and for reasons we have both been honest about. And that is *good*—never think otherwise.' The slightest edge crept into his voice. 'But we can be honest, too, about the flame that burns between us! That, too, is good and honest and true. And why should we not yield to that flame? We are consenting adults, my most beautiful and alluring bride…' His voice had a wry humour in it now. 'So why should we not consent to what we both clearly wish to do?'

She felt him turn her hand in his, lift it to his mouth. He moved his lips across it slowly, sensuously… arousingly…and she felt the flame that his kiss had fired in her flicker in her senses.

'Why should we not consent?' he said again, turning over her hand so that his mouth was moving on her open palm, her delicate, sensitive wrist…

Her blood started to beat up inside her again, her breathing quickening. But it was a breath she must use for a different purpose. To speak—to tell. Before his caresses turned her mind to mush and that urgent hunger leapt in her body again…that hunger she had never known before.

'Because…' Her voice was low, barely audible, and her eyes were barely able to meet his, even in the dim of the night. 'Because I have never—'

His mouth lifted from her wrist and she drew her hand from his slackened grip. He stared at her, not understanding. She had to make him understand. *Had* to…

'I never have, Leon,' she said, her voice lower still, though she forced it to be steady.

She dropped her eyes again, unable to look at him. Her hands twisted in her lap. Her stomach clenched and her whole body was tense, suddenly. Awaiting his response.

It came after a silence that seemed to stretch for ever. 'You are telling me,' she heard him say, his voice expressionless, 'that you are a virgin?'

The word seemed to toll like a bell in the night.

She could not speak. Could only nod.

The silence stretched again and she could bear it no longer. Her eyes lifted to him. His face was shadowed and she could not read it.

She swallowed. 'I'm sorry,' she said. It seemed inadequate, but it was the best she could manage. 'I should… I should have told you…made it clear before I—'

With a sudden movement she jerked to her feet, trying to rush past him, wanting only to get away from him.

But he caught at her hand, getting to his feet as well, taking her other hand, his clasp warm and strong.

He looked down into her face. There was something different in his eyes now—something that made her throat tighten and emotion well up in her. It was an emotion she could not name, but only feel.

Slowly, infinitely slowly, he lowered his head to drop a kiss upon her. Not on her mouth, but her forehead. There was a half-smile on his face that she could not understand.

'It's been a long, long day,' he said. 'And this has all been too much for you. Go to bed,' he said quietly. 'And sleep well. Sleep deeply—and alone.'

His light touch fell away, and he stepped aside to let her go indoors.

On stricken limbs, she did.

CHAPTER EIGHT

OVER BREAKFAST THE next morning, out on the sunny deck, she told him of the romances that had never happened. She tried to make her manner not brisk, but frank—though she'd had to steel herself to talk about such a personal subject, and there were two tell-tale flags of colour high on her cheeks.

'I've dated,' she said, with an air of self-consciousness about her as she helped herself to toast and marmalade, not looking directly at him. 'I've been to films, the theatre, the occasional gig or party, with men who work with my stepfather, who scarcely realise that I'm anything more than simply his stepdaughter, Ellie Peters. But I've never been only her, Leon. And I can never let myself forget that.'

She made herself go on, knowing she had to make him understand. 'Because, you see, when you're a princess you have to be…careful. Other girls my age can afford to be carefree—care*less*, even—but for me, and indeed for my sister…' her voice changed as she thought of Marika's doomed romance with the son of their father's enemy '…an unwise choice can be disastrous. It always seemed safer—wiser—never to get involved.' She took a breath, made herself look at him. 'So I didn't.'

Even as she spoke she was conscious of her evasion. Everything she was telling him was true—but it was not all the truth.

I wanted to wait—wait for 'the one'—the man I would love for ever, who would love me in return. It would have made things...simpler.

But how could she say that to this man whom she had married without any love at all?

She lifted her buttered toast and marmalade and looked across at Leon. She gave a little shrug—almost a defiant one. 'So, there it is, Leon.'

She looked away again, lowering her toast to her plate, and suddenly sitting very still, as if she were fighting for composure.

What would he say? How would he reply to what she'd confided to him?

The man who was sitting opposite her was her husband but still so very much a stranger. A man about whom her thoughts—ever since that kiss at their betrothal ball, ever since she had first set eyes on him, ever since that kiss last night—had been so confused.

As they still were.

Her gaze went back to him, unconsciously anxious for his reaction.

Leon made no immediate reply, marshalling the thoughts in his head. What she had told him, and the reasons she had given, made sense. He had thought—assumed—that once they were married they would both yield, with mutual desire, to the flame that burned so strongly between them. Two consenting adults, just as he had told her, happy to consent.

I thought it would be very simple…

But it was far more complicated than that—far more…delicate. And he must get it right…make his reply to her now with utmost care.

'I appreciate completely what you have said, and I thank you, truly, for trusting me sufficiently to tell me.'

His voice was serious, respectful, acknowledging what she'd confided in him, but he smiled across at her—a warm, reassuring smile—saw the tension in her face ease a fraction and was glad. He felt that strange emotion again—felt a resolve forming in him that, whatever it took, he would guide her forward in this journey they would be making together.

I will be her first—her very first!

A sense of wonder struck him and his eyes rested on her again, more warmly still. Then, wanting to banish the last of that tension in her eyes, with a deliberately relaxed movement he reached for his coffee cup, made his voice as relaxed, too.

'So, tell me, what would you like to do today? Do you want to go out on the water? The lake looks very calm—shall we give it a go?'

He saw her eyelashes flicker for a moment, and then she returned his smile, as if relieved that he was talking about ordinary matters now. And such enjoyable ones.

'Oh, yes—let's!'

There was enthusiasm in her voice, relief, too, he could hear, and Leon was glad.

'We'll order a picnic to take with us as well, shall we?' he went on.

There was equal enthusiasm for that notion, and he knew he had set the right tone for the day ahead. He would take the H from honeymoon and make it stand for holiday instead.

His eyes rested on her, though his gaze was veiled. How incredibly beautiful she was! Her face was lit by the morning sun, minimal make-up, and she wore an open-necked short-sleeved shirt over short-cropped cotton trousers. There was a string of colourful beads around her neck, no more adornment than that, and yet she took his breath away.

Resolve filled him once more, and that same unknown emotion came yet again.

I must not rush her—it must be in her own time—only when she is truly ready to accept what is between us.

It was going to be a self-denying abstinence, but he knew he absolutely had to let her be comfortable with him…take everything at the pace she could cope with.

'I'll row. You steer,' said Leon, offering his hand to help Ellie into the rowing boat by the jetty, then seating himself and pushing off with one of the oars. 'Here goes!' he said cheerfully.

Cheerfulness was going to be his watchword. Cheerfulness, friendliness and easy-going companionship. That was what was needed now, and he would give it willingly. And it seemed to be working, for his bride, who had fled from him the night before, was now matching his cheerful demeanour in equal measure, and that gave him satisfaction enough for now.

*She has to get used to me. Has to become at ease
with me.*

That was essential. Right now it was obvious to him
that she simply could not cope with the intense physical intimacy that had burst into flame between them
the night before—it had been too much, too soon. And
for a reason that he had never dreamt of...

He felt again the echo of the shock he'd felt when
he'd realised what it was she had been telling him last
night. It was not, he knew, something he'd ever have
thought about her—or any woman her age. She was
twenty-six, after all, and had led far less of a sheltered
life than her sister, still cocooned in the royal palace in
Karylya. It would have been natural to assume she'd
had romances in her adult life, and with her incandes-
cent beauty, her outgoing personality and confident experience of the real world, thanks to her upbringing,
anything else would have been unusual in the extreme.

Yet those romances had never happened. She had
told him as much And it was to that end that he was
now being so cheerful and easy-going, pulling strongly
at the oars, heading across the lake.

Though he gave no sign that he had noticed, he had
seen with satisfaction how her gaze flickered over his
torso as he rowed, his muscles visibly flexing under
the T-shirt he was sporting. It was a regard he returned
in spades, drinking in the way her long bare legs were
slanting across the hollow of the boat, her elbows resting
on the gunwale, the sun kissing her face as he longed
to do...

He speeded up his rowing. Vigorous exercise would
be a sensible diversion from such longings.

* * *

Ellie settled herself on one of the rattan chairs on the sunny deck with a pleasurable sigh. It had been, she thought, a lovely day—just lovely! They had reached a tiny islet, dragged the rowing boat ashore, and made a mini-camp to enjoy their hearty picnic. She had fed the left-over pastry crumbs from their raised game pies to a suddenly attentive family of wild ducks—'Malcolm would disapprove, but I can't resist…and besides, it's to say thank you for invading their haven here!' she'd laughed—and then it had been her turn to take the oars, weaving a meandering course towards a jetty on the far side of the lake.

They'd moored up there and had gone ashore to explore the woods, with Ellie telling Leon what she knew of forest ecology and the wildlife it sheltered. There had been a path of sorts, but Leon had helped her over fallen branches, his hand strong and firm, his clasp nothing more than helpful.

Relief was uppermost in her. How much easier it was to have him the way he was being now—cheerful and relaxed, interested in what she was telling him, a convivial and easy-going companion. Oh, she was still constantly aware of his magnetic physical appeal, but she would set that aside for now. It was easier that way…

I've married a man who was all but a stranger on our wedding day—but now I want to get used to being with him, get to know him…spend time with him that is simple, easy. Without any complications…

She felt her mind sheer away from just what such 'complications' might be—they were too much to cope with. Now she just wanted to go on being the way they'd been today. Uncomplicated. Enjoyable. Very pleasantly enjoyable. And for that she was grateful.

He's easy to be with.

It was a good thought to have about the man she had married to protect her father and his family. He was sitting down opposite her now, unfolding a map of the estate as she poured out their tea.

'It's not open to the public at the moment, so we can roam wherever we want,' he was saying. 'We can visit the big house, too, if you like. Plus, there are cycle trails everywhere, with bikes provided.' He paused, then quirked an eyebrow at her. 'Does that all sound very tame?' he asked.

Ellie shook her head firmly. 'No, it sounds totally relaxing—and that is just what I want.' She glanced at him. 'Are you sure *you* won't be bored?'

As she spoke she felt colour mount in her cheeks. She knew Leon had had very different intentions for their stay here.

If he saw her start to flush, he gave no sign of it. 'I haven't been on a bike since I was a kid,' he said ruminatively.

'Me neither!' Ellie laughed, glad her flush was subsiding.

They pored over the map together, working out the best trails, and apart from catching the heady scent of Leon's aftershave, and noticing that at this hour of the day his chiselled jawline was roughening with regrowth, she coped with it admirably. Leon seemed unaware of her covert observation of him, and she was grateful.

She was grateful, too, that he continued to be cheerful and easy-going all through dinner and beyond. It had started to drizzle, so they settled down by the fire in the sitting room, watching a history documentary on TV. Leon stretched his long legs out towards the fire as he nursed a cognac at the other end of the sofa from her, and Ellie sipped a glass of sweet dessert wine.

It was easy, it was comfortable, it was companionable. And the same comfortable, companionable ease continued over the leisurely days that followed.

They made their cycling expedition—top-brand bikes having been delivered to the cottage after breakfast—whizzing along leafy forest trails and ending up at a Victorian mansion designed by a notable Gothic Revival architect for an exhaustive tour.

'An acquired taste,' Ellie said tactfully, more used to the delicately gilded rococo style of her father's palace or the medieval north country fastness of her uncle's principal seat.

They also explored the area by car. There was a race circuit nearby, and Ellie insisted Leon indulge in a track session, watching him with a stab of alarm at the terrifying speeds he coaxed from his beloved supercar—an alarm he laughed off afterwards with airy unconcern and post-race exhilaration. And she also sensed an air of satisfaction that she should have felt alarmed for him in the first place.

They added in a visit to a ruined abbey in a nearby river valley, sad and atmospheric, where one of the Romantics had once penned an equally sad and atmospheric sonnet, which Ellie had had to learn by heart at school, and quoted verbatim as they walked around the ruins.

They'd headed for a nearby scenic market town, where they browsed in second-hand bookshops and indulged in a pub lunch of fish and chips—only bettered by a lavish cream tea the following day, at a quaint tea shop in a picture-postcard traditional English village thronged with tourists taking photos of rose-covered thatched cottages and the well-stocked duck pond.

As they sat at their tiny table in the bay window, over-looking the village green, Leon listened to Ellie chatting amiably to the family sitting at the next table about the picturesque village.

When the other family left, he spoke. 'Do you never worry you'll be recognised?' he asked curiously.

She shook her head. 'Not really. Even those people who've heard of Karylya won't think a daughter of the ex-sovereign would be having tea here!' She gave a laugh, and pointed to where his sleek, low-slung car was parked outside. 'That monster of yours is getting far more attention than me!' she said.

A group of young lads and their dads were clustered admiringly around Leon's car and Leon, adopting his bride's own friendly attitude, found himself chatting to them as he and Ellie prepared to leave.

Exchanging performance data with those whose knowledge of top-marque vehicles way exceeded any hope of ever being able to afford one themselves, he amiably let them take selfies with the car, then gunned the powerful engine with a satisfyingly loud roar just for them, before finally heading off with a casual wave of his hand.

Ellie strapped herself into the passenger seat, smiling at Leon for what he'd just done. Her thoughts were warm.

I scarcely knew him when I married him—but now that I am getting to know him, how much there is to like!

Emotion fluttered in her.

To be so devastatingly good-looking and yet to be so good-natured with it!

It was a rare combination.

That flutter of emotion came again…

'That was so nice of you!' said Ellie. 'You could see how thrilled those boys were!'

The warmth of her thoughts was in her voice, and Leon turned his head towards her.

'Just following your example,' he said, and smiled.

It warmed him to hear the warmth in her voice, to see it in her eyes on him.

And he felt his longing for her ache through him…

'Do you know, we've been here a week already?' Ellie mused.

They were taking their customary after-dinner liqueur out on the deck. The sky tonight was clear, and starlight glittered on the dark surface of the lake. Her thoughts were strange. The week had passed so swiftly, and as each day had passed she had felt more and more at ease with Leon. He was a stranger no longer—

But if not a stranger—then what?

The question hung in her head—but she could give herself no answer.

She was glad when he spoke. 'I think that calls for a toast!' he said, and smiled, raising his glass accordingly.

* * *

Behind his smile, he rested his eyes on her as they stood by the railing, breathing in the soft night air.

Was she a little closer to him than she usually stood?

The scent of her perfume caught at him and desire flared. How incredibly beautiful she was! How enchantingly so!

How I ache for her...

Had something of his longing for her shown in his eyes as their glasses touched? It must have, because there was a sudden answering flare in her eyes...

Then her eyes dropped and she turned her face away to look out over the water. There seemed to be a new tension in her stance.

Deliberately, he let the moment pass. And he made his voice nothing more than casual as he spoke again. 'So, has it been a good week?' he enquired.

She turned to look at him. Her expression was glowing. 'Wonderful!' she answered.

She seemed to hold his eyes for a moment, as if she wanted to say something else but was unsure. Leon waited. Every instinct on alert.

Her eyes searched his face. 'I want to thank you,' she said, her voice low. 'Not just for bringing me here—for knowing that this place is just what I needed! But...but for so much else, Leon. For being so understanding.'

There was an intensity in her voice he had never heard before, and he felt himself respond. He knew the meaning of what she was saying—knew there was only one answer he could give her.

'You must know,' he said, 'that whatever you choose—or do not choose—I will abide by it.'

Her eyes were searching his. Something was working in her face that he had never seen before.

'You're being very good about it, Leon,' she said. 'Many men would have—' She broke off, not sure what word to use.

Leon supplied one. 'Sulked?' he suggested, not hiding the tug of humour at his mouth.

She gave a lip-biting laugh. 'Oh, dear, yes—perhaps!' She glanced up at him. 'But somehow, you know, you're not the sulking type, I think!'

Ellie had said it humorously, conscious, with a strange little flurry of awareness, that she'd also said it teasingly…almost flirtatiously…

She wanted to break her glance away, and yet, feeling again that same little flurry, she didn't. She held his gaze for a moment longer. Had something changed in his eyes, too? She wasn't sure—could only feel that flurry stirring inside her again, that same low vibration in her blood that had started up the first time they'd stood here like this, at the water's edge, under the night sky.

She dropped her eyes, finding it too disturbing, and let her gaze go out over the darkling waters of the lake. Thoughts stirred within her…feelings and emotions she knew she must make sense of.

But how?

What certainties were hers?

One above all.

He can arouse in me a response that no other man has ever drawn from me. A single glance from him can make me tremble...a single touch can set my every sense aflame...

She had fled from that flame, confused and overwhelmed. Unable to cope with it. But in the week that had passed he had given her time and space to think again.

She had married without love—but had she married without passion, without desire? She could give no answer but the truth. The truth that Leon had spelt out to her—the same flame burned in both of them...

She turned her head, looking at him again. He was standing very still, as if giving her time, letting her think the thoughts that filled her head. She felt the familiar catch in her throat that came every time she looked at him, drank in the strong planed features of the face she could never willingly tear her eyes from...

The strength of it shook her.

The strength of her desire for him.

More thoughts came—thoughts that she had to frame and answer.

Two years they would be together—no more than that. Then she would be free to leave, to find the true love she sought.

But until then, would desire suffice?

Perhaps I am safe because there will only ever be desire between us. Because that is all he wants. For is it not what I want, too?

She had never been free to indulge her senses, but Leon was no passing boyfriend who might simply prove an unwise choice if their relationship soured. Leon was her husband—and he had shown patience and understanding, shown himself to be someone she could be at ease with, find companionship with, enjoy the hours she spent with him.

And he was the man she desired.

The man I want to give myself to—and take in return—

Surely it would be safe to yield to her desire for such a man?

The knowledge filled her, removing all doubt, all confusion. Making all clear to her.

She spoke his name, low and soft.

She saw something change in his expression—as if, she realised, he had been holding himself on a tight leash—a leash he had now loosened.

He lifted his hand, then paused, and she could sense he was exerting absolute control in doing so.

His eyes searched hers in the dim starlight. 'I don't want to scare you away again.'

CHAPTER NINE

Leon's voice was low. Intensity filled him, but he fought against letting it show. Every instinct told him that it was happening—that what he had yearned for all this long, long week, yearned for since the moment he had first set eyes on her, was now happening.

But it must be at her pace—and hers alone. His desire must remain leashed until she was ready to release it.

He felt his heart start to beat in heavy, insistent slugs. Desire was building in him—filling him…

Slowly, very slowly, she turned her head.

'I could stay here all night,' she murmured. 'Watch the stars set and the sunrise…'

She looked out over the glimmering surface of the lake, relaxing against the railing, aware that the movement would bring her closer to him, brushing his shoulder with hers.

She felt his arm go around her, drawing her closer still. It was warm and she leaned into him, feeling his strength and solidity supporting her.

It felt good.

Right.

She breathed in the sweet night air, felt the waft of the light night wind winnowing the tendrils of her hair, teasing at her cheek, the sensitive nape of her neck.

She caught the musky, masculine scent of him, the potent maleness of him.

It felt good.

Right.

The fingers of his hand started to play lightly on her bare upper arm, idly. She gave a sigh at the languorous pleasure it aroused, leaning into him even more.

She felt the drift of his lips across the crown of her hair, heard him murmur something to her in Greek. Husky and low.

She lifted her face to his, searching the gaze fixed on her. Reached with her free hand to his jaw, roughened at this late hour. Let her fingertips move slowly along the hard edge of his jaw, across the sculpted outline of his mouth…

In her veins, a pulse started to beat. Warmth was filling her, and there was a quickening in her senses. She felt desire pool in her, gathering strength, deepening in intensity.

She turned her body into his, sliding her hand around the strong nape of his neck, into the feathered sable of his hair, and his hand dropped to her waist, wrapping around it.

She could feel the desire inside her strengthen, become a yearning, an ache she could not still or banish. She could only give herself to it, fully and freely…

She said his name again, raising her mouth to his, kissing him softly, with infinite care.

He did not kiss her back, he did not move in any

way, but he let her lips touch his, as if daring her to take such liberties with him. As if testing what she was doing and why.

And as her mouth moved slowly, exploring his, as she felt that sweet, languorous arousal welling up within her, she knew and had never been more sure of anything in her life that it glowed within her like a bright flame of truth—that this moment now was right—that being here, with Leon, with this man she had married, the man she desired, was right...

Desire, warm and sweet and overwhelming, swept through her, deepening her kiss, and as it did so it seemed to light an answering flame in him. And all of a sudden it was not just her kissing him, but Leon catching her mouth, her lips, parting them with his with a sudden urgency that was like a match thrown onto tinder.

She drowned in it, the blood leaping in her, a smothered cry in her throat, and then her hand at his nape was shaping itself to him, her other hand sliding across the broad, muscled front of his torso, glorying in the strength she found there.

He crushed her to him and the cry in her throat came again, filled with wonder and longing.

Instantly his mouth released her and his hands cupped her face. In the dim night, his eyes burned gold.

'Are you *sure*, Ellie? You must be absolutely sure! If—if this isn't what you want, you must say so now... *now*.' His expression changed. 'It would be agony for me to let you go again. I long for you so much!'

His voice was hoarse, his eyes dark and strained.

'I have given you time—the time I knew you needed.

One Minute" Survey

You get TWO books <u>and</u> TWO Mystery Gifts...

Dear Reader,

Your opinions are important to us. So if you'll participate in our fast and free "One Minute" Survey, **YOU** can pick two wonderful books that **WE** pay for!

As a leading publisher of women's fiction, we'd love to hear from you. That's why we promise to reward you for completing our survey.

IMPORTANT: Please complete the survey and return it. We'll send your Free Books and Free Mystery Gifts right away. **And we pay for shipping and handling too!**

Thank you again for participating in our "One Minute" Survey. It really takes just a minute (or less) to complete the survey… and your free books and gifts will be well worth it!

↖ *We pay for EVERYTHING!*

Sincerely,

Pam Powers

Pam Powers
for Reader Service

"One Minute" Survey

GET YOUR FREE BOOKS AND FREE GIFTS!

✓ Complete this Survey ✓ Return this survey

▶ DETACH AND MAIL CARD TODAY! ▶

1 Do you try to find time to read every day?
☐ YES ☐ NO

2 Do you prefer stories with happy endings?
☐ YES ☐ NO

3 Do you enjoy having books delivered to your home?
☐ YES ☐ NO

4 Do you find a Larger Print size easier on your eyes?
☐ YES ☐ NO

YES! I have completed the above "One Minute" Survey. Please send me my Two Free Books and Two Free Mystery Gifts (worth over $20 retail). I understand that I am under no obligation to buy anything, as explained on the back of this card.

❏ I prefer the regular-print edition
106/306 HDL GNPG

❏ I prefer the larger-print edition
176/376 HDL GNPG

FIRST NAME	LAST NAME

ADDRESS

APT.#	CITY

STATE/PROV.	ZIP/POSTAL CODE

READER SERVICE—Here's how it works:

▲ If offer card is missing write to: Reader Service, P.O. Box 1341, Buffalo, NY 14240-8531 or visit www.ReaderService.com ▼

BUSINESS REPLY MAIL
FIRST-CLASS MAIL   PERMIT NO. 717   BUFFALO, NY

POSTAGE WILL BE PAID BY ADDRESSEE

READER SERVICE
PO BOX 1341
BUFFALO NY 14240-8571

NO POSTAGE
NECESSARY
IF MAILED
IN THE
UNITED STATES

But if it's not yet right, if it never will be right, then tell me now…'

His voice seemed to crack, and it drew from her an answering choke. Her eyes clung to his, her hands now closing around the strong muscles of his upper arm as if to steady herself with his strength.

Her face turned upwards to his. 'This *is* the time, Leon,' she said. 'I want this… I want *you*.' The catch came in her voice again. 'Oh, Leon, I want this, and you, and everything—*everything*!'

Her hands spasmed on his arms, clenching them tightly, glorying in their muscled strength, glorying in his closeness, in the heady scent of him, the heat of his body so close to hers. Glorying in everything!

I'm glorying in him…in the man I want…desire…as I have never wanted any other! This man that I have married. Leon—my husband.

And it seemed to her the most wonderful thing in all the world that he was her husband.

He needed no other answer. No other reassurance. Nothing else to stop him doing what he wanted with every fibre of his being to do now.

He lifted her into his arms. She was as light as a feather, drifting down to the darkened surface of the lake to float upon the water, and her arms wrapped around his neck.

He gazed down at her. 'And I will give you everything…'

That husk was in his voice, and the gold blaze of his eyes was molten.

He strode indoors and she let herself be carried by him. She could resist him no more. Could not resist the overpowering response to him that she had tried to ignore, and then deny, and then be fearful of. But he had overcome her fears.

His name was on her lips and he paused on the stairs to drop the swiftest kiss upon her, as if to answer her, and then he was taking her into his room, lowering her down upon the bed as gently as if she were fragile porcelain.

He stood back, and in the dim light she realised he was swiftly, urgently peeling his clothes from himself, exercising the most ruthless self-control as he did so. Then, gloriously, he was coming down beside her, and whilst her eyes widened instinctively as the lean, naked strength of his body was revealed to her—along with the evidence of his desire for her—suddenly she had to turn her head away, as if it were a sight too much for her. She could feel heat beating up in her, like a kindled furnace racing flames through her veins.

The weight of his body beside her dipped the mattress and her body rolled to his as his hand reached out to clasp hers, while the other hand gently, inexorably, turned her head towards him.

He was propped on one elbow, looking down at her. 'I can't hide my desire from you,' he said. His voice was low, intent. 'I want you so much… I ache for you…'

His strong fingers were warm on her cheek as she gazed up at him, the breath tight in her lungs, her heart thumping beneath her ripened breasts, which were straining at the material of her top. Her own evidence of her aching desire for him…

'And now, my most beautiful, beautiful bride, we can share all there is between us—all our desire.'

He paused, and she saw again the absolute self-control he was exerting. She said his name, and as she did so it was as if that iron self-control was released. With a rasp in his throat, he brought his mouth down on hers again, and this time there was no urgency, only slow, sensual desire designed to arouse, to draw from her with every silken glide the quickening of her own desire.

It melted through her, feeding the hunger that now rose in her—a hunger not just for his mouth, his lips and tongue, but for so much more of him. For all of him.

But to have all of him—all of that powerful, glorious body beside her—she must divest herself of what separated them. Restlessly, still beneath his silken mouth, she moved her legs, as if to free herself of the folds of her dress. Then his hand was on her thigh, performing that very office for her, and with a sudden movement, a low laugh, he had lifted himself from her, flipping her over with an effortless twist.

'You must allow me to do what it will be my exquisite pleasure to do,' he informed her, and his voice was nothing more than a husk, his eyes glinting in the dim light.

And allow him she did. She let his hand move to the zip at the back of her dress and slide it slowly, achingly, down, exposing the graceful curve of her spine. With the slightest movement of his hand he had also unfastened her bra, she realised, and now, as she gave a gasp, he was peeling both dress and bra from her supine body, casually lifting her hips to allow him to slide it from her completely.

She gave another gasp, for somehow her panties had

disappeared with the other clothes, and with burning consciousness she realised that she was lying there, her body naked to his view and to the sensuous stroke of his fingertips…

A sigh went through her. A sigh of bliss and pleasure as slowly, making indulgent trails and whorls, he explored the contours of her back, from the delicate nape of her neck, down the long elegant sculpture of her spine, to the ripe roundness of her hips and the sweet mound below.

She felt her fingers sink into the bedding, heard herself give a long, languorous sigh, heard his low, husky laugh as she did so.

Yet even as she sighed at the sweet, sensuous pleasure of his touch, she knew it was not enough. A hunger was building in her, an ache, a longing… A restlessness… She felt her legs moving, scissoring, her hips flexing.

In instinctive answer to her need, Leon rolled her over again, and with another gasp she realised she was gazing up at him now, her body exposed to his. She heard him say something in Greek—a low growl whose words she did not know but whose meaning she did.

A kind of glory filled her as she lay there. For the very first time in her life a man was gazing upon her nakedness, and she knew that her nakedness was for him alone, only for him. Only for Leon…

She lifted her arms to loop them around his neck—but not to draw him down to her, only to raise her breasts to him, ripe and swollen, their peaks cresting. She was offering herself to him. And his mouth was lowering to them, his lips coming around one and then the other, and the pleasure of it consumed her, made her cry out.

Her spine was arching now, as his hands shaped the swell of her breasts, feasting on them. There was an urgency now in his movements, in his mouth as its touch drew from her a quickening of her flesh. She moved again, that hunger, that restlessness consuming her. She wanted more…and yet more. She wanted everything—everything he could give her, bestow upon her.

She felt his body lower to hers—felt with yet another gasp how strong and powerful his manhood was, pressing upon her. Instinctively, with a knowledge as old as time itself, she slackened her thighs, opening her body to his. He was kissing her mouth now, feasting upon it as he had upon her ripened breasts. She felt her hips lifting to his in invitation, with a hunger that came from the very core of her being.

And yet he drew back, though with a little cry she tried to hold him.

'Not yet—' That rasp of absolute self-control was in his voice again. 'Not yet,' he urged again, his mouth against hers, 'or I will hurt you. And I would give all the world not to!' He brushed his mouth against hers. 'Trust me—trust me on this.' There was a smile in his voice now. 'Be patient…'

'I can't!' she cried, her voice breathless, infused with the urgency that was filling her body. 'I can't! I want you so much, Leon—I didn't know… I didn't realise how this would be!'

Her legs moved again, that restless hunger consuming her. Her hand grasped at his hip, seeking to draw him down on her again, to feel the hard pleasure of his body upon hers, to open herself to him, to his possession.

But her restless movement was stilled. His palm was on her abdomen, splayed out, holding her still.

'Wait,' he said. 'It will be better for you this way— *trust me.*'

There was a command in his voice, but somewhere deep within herself she did not mind. She wanted to give herself to him, she ached to do so with all her being, but he had asked her to trust him and trust him she would.

And then, as his palm slid downwards into the vee of her thighs, she realised that everything up till this moment had been only the *hors d'oeuvre* before the banquet of the senses he was giving her.

Her hand spasmed on his shoulder and her head fell back, a gasp coming from her that silenced all that had come before. 'Oh, sweet heaven…'

Had she spoken aloud? Perhaps… For he had given that low, seductive laugh again, and dropped a soft, sensual kiss on her mouth.

'Sweet heaven,' he said huskily, 'is exactly where I am going to take you.'

Her eyes fluttered shut. Sensations so exquisite she could not believe the human body could experience them quivered through her as his skilled fingertips sought and found her tender folds. She felt her spine arch again, heard low, helpless gasps break from her as the pleasure he engendered mounted and mounted and mounted, until it was unbearable…just unbearable…

'Leon… I can't… I can't…'

The soft kiss came again. 'Then don't,' he said.

'Don't fight it, my most beautiful, beautiful one. This… *this* is for you…'

One last sweet touch, one last, sweet pressure, one last pang of unbearably exquisite hunger…and then flame sheeted through her. An inferno of flame, lifting and burning her, consuming her, turning her body to liquid fire. She was threshing her limbs, moving her head upon the pillow, her spine arching like a bow. She cried out in glory and in wonder, in an ecstasy whose existence she had never even glimpsed. Her body was pulsing, convulsing…

And then, with a sudden movement, Leon's body was over hers, fusing with hers, and they were becoming one flesh, melded together, and he was surging within her, strongly and powerfully. A cry broke from him, deep and low, and her hands clawed over his shoulders. His hands snaked around her hips, lifting her to him, and her thighs locked around him. He threw his head back, the powerful sinews of his neck exposed, the pulse at his throat surging with the intensity of his release.

Time stopped. Eternity started. An eternity of ecstasy that brought sobs from her throat.

Her arms cradled him to her as ecstasy turned to weeping, emotion overpowering her, overwhelming her. He was rocking her in his arms, saying her name over and over again, and still she sobbed.

He drew back from her, though she tried to keep him with her.

'Ellie, have I hurt you? *Have I hurt you?*' Horror was in his voice.

She did not answer—could not. She only pulled him back to her, and he let her…let her pull his head onto her shoulder, let her arms hug him to her as if she would never let him go. And as her body slowly stilled he realised, with a flood of gratitude and relief, that her tears were not from pain…

His arms came around her, turning her so that it was now she who lay cradled in his arms. He hauled her to him, stroking his hand down the long, tangled tresses of her hair, his voice soothing her, calming her, quietening her as her trembling body eased and stilled.

And still he stroked her hair, murmuring the words that she needed to hear and he needed to speak. Until her body was quiet in his embrace and the sweet lassitude of passion spent swept over them both and sleep possessed them—as they had possessed each other in the glory and ecstasy of their union.

CHAPTER TEN

SLOWLY, ELLIE MOVED. Rousing herself from the depths of a slumber so profound it seemed to have taken her to a distant world. Slowly, she lifted heavy eyelids, blinking in the sunlight that streamed through the uncurtained window. The pillow her head was resting on seemed to be flexing, shifting position, and she realised with a rush of dawning consciousness that it was not a pillow, but a shoulder... Leon's shoulder.

He moved again, lifted his head now, and his lips brushed hers softly and tenderly. 'Good morning...'

There was a smile in the murmur, and a smile in the deep, dark eyes pouring into hers. And in the ordinary words of greeting there was the sweetness of intimacy that brought memory rushing in upon her.

She did not answer him—could not. Could only lie there, gazing up at him, quite helpless to do anything else. Not wanting to do anything else. Her heart was rich and full, and she was in the only place in the whole world she wanted to be! In Leon's arms.

How wonderful he'd made it for her—and how right, how absolutely *right* it had been, that it was Leon who had taken her on that journey she had never taken before. Her eyes glowed with all she felt.

'Now, that,' Leon murmured, 'is a look worth getting up for in the morning!' He made his voice light, with laughter in it—but there was a lot more than laughter.

No woman had ever gazed at him like that, with everything in her eyes…

He felt a warmth start to fill him—as if… A thought came to him, strange but powerful, as if something frozen deep inside him was thawing. He found himself wondering at it… It was as if something he had held on to for too long—so many years—was melting away from him. But what it was he did not know.

He had known it would be special between them—his desire for her had been so instant, so overpowering from the moment he'd first seen her—but more than that it had been special because of what she'd told him. That he would be the very first to show her all that could be between a man and woman.

But is it even more than that?

His eyes searched her face…so beautiful. Her eyes were gazing up at him, and he felt again that strange sense of something thawing deep inside him. It was disquieting, disturbing, and he was glad when a smile broke across her face, dispelling those thoughts he could give no name to, no reason for, and she gave an answering laugh to his, her eyes warm upon him.

He dropped a kiss on the tip of her delicate nose. 'Time for breakfast,' he told her.

For himself, he would have lingered all morning here in bed with her, but he knew he must not indulge himself—he had been as gentle as he could with her, and he must be considerate still.

'I could demolish—what is it you call it?—a full English!'

Which was exactly what he did some twenty minutes later—a whole pile of bacon and sausages and fried eggs and tomatoes and mushrooms, and a mountain of fried bread—out on the sunny deck, watched by Ellie with a smile of doting indulgence on her face as she delicately crunched toast and marmalade.

Replete, finally, Leon pushed his empty plate away. 'Right,' he said. 'I'm ready to start the day. What shall we do?'

He knew exactly what *he* wanted to do, but that was out of the question. Time, instead, for some more diversion. Energetic diversion, preferably.

'Shall we take the rowing boat out again?' he ventured.

'Oh, yes, please!' came her immediate answer, her face lighting up. 'And another picnic lunch on that little islet?'

'Whatever you want,' Leon promised her. 'Absolutely whatever you want…'

His gaze rested on her, warm and golden.

My princess bride—my very own princess bride! Made mine at last.

In the days that followed, in the same easy-going way of those days they'd spent together already, the intimacy of passion and desire that he had craved—as she, too, did now, he thought—they seemed to be bathed in a kind of perpetual golden light.

Which was odd, really, for the sunny weather they'd had since the wedding had broken, and rain swept in from the west, drumming on the lake, on the deck, on the windows of the cottage.

But Leon was glad of it—grateful for it.

For now, indoors, hunkered down by a roaring fire, toasting muffins on long forks or lolling on the sofa, drinking champagne, their arms around each other, watching rom-coms and thrillers and anything else that took their fancy on the TV, it really was as if the rest of the world simply no longer existed.

And that suited him fine—just fine.

Oh, soon he would be showing Ellie off to the world—his radiant princess bride!—but right now all he wanted was simply to revel in having her entirely to himself. This was new to him, he knew, being constantly with a single woman. And it felt good—very good indeed.

As he gazed down at her now, snuggled up to him on the sofa as the rain lashed down outside, he felt again that same strange feeling that had come to him as he'd woken that first morning with her in his arms, as if something were thawing deep inside him. And with it came that same feeling of disquiet...

Deliberately, to dispel that strange feeling, he bent his head to brush her mouth with his, letting his lips glide sensuously, arousingly, across hers. He felt her mouth respond, move against his, deepening the kiss. His hand closed over the sweet mound of her ripening breast and he felt his own body quicken...

Making love, he discovered, beside an open fire, on a soft deep hearthrug, was a blissfully pleasurable experience, sating him completely...banishing all disquieting thoughts.

He kept them banished—they had no place in his marriage. Not in the glittering marriage he had made to crown the achievements of his life, obtaining for himself a wife whose royal blood flowed in the veins of the most beautifully alluring woman he had ever known, whose embrace fired in him an intensity of desire that flared between them every time...

And it continued to do so, just as intensely, in the weeks that followed, even after they'd left the haven of their honeymoon cottage and set off into the wider world again. A world which welcomed them with open arms and showered invitations down upon them as they embarked upon an exhaustive round of every fashionable high-society event in the social calendar so that he could be seen with her.

He revelled in it all, and the radiantly beautiful Princess Elizsaveta—his wife, his bride!—made an entrance wherever she went, *en grande tenue*.

They were photographed and fêted, deluged with invitations to balls and dances, to house parties and yacht parties, beach parties and polo parties—every kind of glittering gathering of the highest of high society. They had become the most glamorous, fashionable newlyweds in Europe and beyond.

It was a world away from the life Ellie had lived with either of her parents, in very different ways—whether with her mother, accompanying her stepfather on location, or with her father at the royal palace in Karylya. But with Leon at her side she gave herself to it all—to the non-stop hectic whirl of endless socialising, dressed in couture gowns, adorned with jewellery and every chic accessory she possessed. To make herself beautiful for Leon. To dazzle the world for him…

Leon.

Her gaze went to him now, as they strolled companionably along the terrace above the marina in Monte Carlo. They'd just come from a lavish bash on one of the multi-million-pound yachts moored below, and the hour was late.

She felt desire quicken within her. How effortlessly fabulous he looked, as he always did, in a superbly fitting tuxedo, moulding his tall, muscled body, with his loosened tie giving him a raffish look, as did the edge of regrowth along his jawline.

Her stomach gave a little flip, anticipating what would come when they were back in their hotel suite.

The intensity of her desire—the desire his touch always unleashed in her—washed through her. It had swept her away—*he* had swept her away!—into a world she had never known, of physical desire and sensual bliss.

She slipped her hand into his, rejoicing in the strength of his clasp, the warmth of his fingers meshing with hers. She was eager to get back to their suite. To have Leon all to herself, to take him into her arms and to feel that sweet, eager desire released in her…

But even as she felt the rush of desire flushing through her, something stayed her.

What they had, she and Leon, was a comfortable camaraderie in the day and a burning ecstasy in the night. By day, friends. By night…lovers. Lovers fuelled by an intensity of passion that burned between them without quenching.

A sense of restlessness possessed her suddenly. These weeks with Leon had been wonderful, an adventure she had embraced as they had travelled across Europe and beyond to wherever the jet set roamed and gathered, living it up by day and by night, dressed to the nines whatever the time of day, looking her very best for Leon. But it was a rootless existence, staying in hotels or other people's homes. Always with people all around them.

She felt a longing to be done with it—at least for a while. To have Leon to herself again, as she had on their honeymoon. Simple days…and searing nights.

Because if she did—if she had Leon entirely to herself—then perhaps…

Perhaps something more could grow between them—something more than friendship and desire…

Is that what I want? More than what I have now with Leon?

The question plucked at her, seeking an answer. An answer she could not give.

She broke off her thoughts. Leon had paused in their strolling, and was looking out over the marina. She welcomed the diversion from her sudden restlessness.

'So, what do you think—shall we hire a yacht for ourselves?' He turned to glance at her.

The idea beguiled her. She pointed to a yacht that was considerably smaller than most of the others, but looked leaner and faster. It also looked as if it wouldn't need a crew.

We could be alone together on it and sail off into the

sunset, she thought wistfully. *Away from all the crowds and the people and the parties. We could be alone together again, the way we were on our honeymoon... just Leon and me...*

A yearning filled her to have Leon all to herself again, but he was speaking.

'Sure you don't want that one?' he quizzed, pointing at a mega-yacht lit up like a Christmas tree, the size of a floating hotel, dwarfing the other yachts and sporting not one, but two helidecks and three underlit swimming pools.

She gave a gurgle of laughter, knowing he wasn't serious, and glad to have her unexpectedly pensive mood lifted by humour. She made some archly disparaging remark about 'vulgar oligarchs' and left it at that.

Leon chuckled and drew her away, strolling with her hand in hand back to their nearby hotel.

His mood was good—very good.

As ever, Ellie had been fêted today, as she always was, wherever he took her, and he'd loved seeing her the cynosure of all eyes, her beauty and natural charm radiant. His glance was warm as he looked upon her in her ivory evening gown, diamonds around her slender throat. How incredibly beautiful she was—and how absolutely and totally *his*!

The two months since their honeymoon had just flashed by, in a whirl of pleasure and travel and hedonistic enjoyment. His vast wealth was being managed by the highly paid professionals he'd appointed, and overseen by himself, so all he had to do now with his money was enjoy it.

With Ellie at his side. His perfect princess bride.

How right I was to marry her—how perfect she is for me!

It was a now-familiar refrain that came to him again, in the small hours of that night, as she lay in his arms in the sensuous aftermath of their slaked desire. This marriage he had made so deliberately, to set the seal on his achievements, was proving even better than he'd anticipated! They were good together, he and his princess bride—comfortably companionable by day, and by night…

Oh, by night she exceeded all his hopes and intentions! He had known from that very first exchange of glances across the penthouse floor lobby, which had signalled their physical responsiveness to each other, that when the time came to claim his bride how good—how *very* good!—it would be. But the reality had been way, way better!

He eased his hand over the soft roundedness of her hip and felt sleep beckon, his thoughts faintly flickering. Was it because he had been the very first man to lead her into the pleasures of intimacy? Or because she was no passing affair but the woman who was his wife, his bride, his dazzling Princess, prized above all other women?

The questions drifted across his slowing thoughts but no answers came. There was only one certainty—the one he lived by and would always live by.

He would never deceive himself—deceive *her*—by calling it by a name that was nothing but a delusion, destructive and dangerous.

No, what drew him to her—and she to him—was

desire. Honest and true, burning between them. He wrapped his arms around her more tightly. *This* was all he wanted—desire, and the slaking of it, with his beautiful, passionate bride. Nothing more.

In his close embrace, her body languorous and sated from the bliss and pleasure still throbbing through her, Ellie felt her hectic heart rate slow and sleep start to creep over her. As it did so, she felt memory start to play in her drowsy thoughts. The memory of how she'd stood on the terrace, overlooking the marina, wanting to sail off into the sunset with Leon…only with him… the man she desired so, so much…

That same sense of yearning filled her now as then, but for what, she didn't know.

Was it the sense of wanting something…*more*?

Ellie reached for the croissant nestling in a silver basket as they breakfasted on their balcony. Below, the yachts moored in the marina were crowded together, mirroring the built-up coastline of this ultra-expensive principality. They were due to attend a reception at the candy-box-pink stucco palace that evening, and Ellie was glad of the invitation for Leon's sake.

But her face shadowed. Being here in Monaco could only be a painful reminder to her of all that her own family had lost for ever.

For a second she was blind to the azure Mediterranean, dazzling beyond the marina—in her mind's eye she saw the snow-capped mountains of Karylya, its verdant forests and lush meadows, the graceful white and gold rococo palace she would never see again. Nor would any of her family...

Had her throat caught? Perhaps it had, for Leon was talking to her, concern in his voice.

'Ellie, what is it?'

She blinked, and the vision of her homeland was gone—but not her yearning for it.

'I'm sorry,' she said. 'I was thinking of Karylya... that I'll never see it again. Thinking of my father...'

She swallowed, her fingers tearing absently at the croissant. She had neglected her parents, she knew, in the months since her wedding, caught up in the hectic social whirl Leon had swept her into. Her mother she felt less bad about—Malcom had taken her to New Zealand and the South Seas, to mix filming with an extended holiday. But her father was having to face his unwelcome new life in exile, in a new home, a new country. And her stepmother and siblings, too—their lives changed just as radically.

On impulse, she spoke. 'Leon—do you think...? Could we visit him?'

Maybe it would do her good—not just to see her father and her half-siblings again, but to take a pause in the social whirl that she and Leon lived in. Take her mind away from that disquieting sense of yearning that hovered about her for the unknown 'more' she could give no name to.

Would give no name to.

She blinked, surfacing from her introspection, and realised that Leon had not answered immediately. That his expression had shuttered.

She swallowed, wishing she had not mentioned it. 'I'm sorry, I shouldn't have asked. You don't want to.'

He gave a shrug of one shoulder. 'Of course we can visit if you want,' he said, but there was a terseness in his voice that she did not miss.

Leon had heard it himself, but did not soften it. He had no wish to see her father again—a man who had been happy to see his daughter marry a complete stranger rather than face poverty for himself. His thoughts darkened. He knew all about fathers who put their own interests above their children's...

'Thank you,' she said awkwardly. 'It's just that I know from Marika's texts that my stepmother is expecting a formal visit from us at some point. And Marika—' She broke off, clearly thinking there was no point in telling Leon she was worried about her sister.

Her eyes were still on him, though.

He had been browsing through glossy yacht brochures, ready to consult the agent that morning about which to hire, but now he set them aside.

'We'll do this another time,' he said. 'Let's visit your father first.'

He did not add, *And get it over with*—that would have been too harsh, and she did not deserve it.

His gaze softened. No, his beautiful princess bride deserved only the best! The best he could bestow upon her!

For an instant, memory thrust at him. His father, presenting his mother with a top fashion label silk scarf, sapphire earrings, a pair of her favourite designer shoes... All with a flourish and a flurry of extravagant declarations of love and devotion. His mother had clapped her hands in excitement and pleasure, telling him he was the most wonderful man in the world, and how she adored him—how he was her whole life…

He slammed the door of memory shut.

He would not allow the past to poison the present.

The present was so very, very good.

His expression softened again. Desire started to rise within him as his gaze rested on Ellie's sunlit face, on a flake of her croissant caught on her lower lip. He reached across the table to brush it off with his thumb, then glided his thumb along the delicate inner surface of her mouth, his eyelids drooping.

He saw her pupils flare, and smiled. His voice was husky with growing arousal. 'Come back to bed…'

He drew her to her feet, and took her there…yielding to the flame of their desire.

All that he wanted…

CHAPTER ELEVEN

LEON'S FACE WAS set as he drove up the poplar-lined avenue leading to the elegant château in the heart of the Loire. He was not looking forward to this visit, and the moment the former Grand Duke and Duchess greeted them, with as much ceremony as if they were still on the throne of Karylya, his mood worsened.

Stilted conversation took place as the royal couple led the way out on to a shaded terrace, where they were served drinks.

'Marika and Niki are playing tennis,' the Grand Duchess informed them. She glanced at Leon. 'The court needed completely resurfacing, alas, and there has, of course, been a great deal of other work required to make everything…' she hesitated briefly '…suitable.'

There was the trace of a sigh in her voice, and Leon found himself bristling. No doubt she was thinking of the palace in Karylya, and all the other royal residences that she no longer possessed now she was reduced to a single château.

Paid for by me.

He cut the thought short. The money he'd spent on

them—was still spending—had brought him Ellie. Was he going to complain about that? Of course not!

His eyes went to her as she said hurriedly, 'And you've made it all absolutely beautiful!'

Her stepmother smiled her gracious smile. 'We've worked extremely hard,' she murmured.

Leon said nothing. He doubted the Grand Duchess had done so much as lift a paint pot with her own fair hands...

'Indeed,' her husband was corroborating her story. 'For myself, I have been starting a library here.'

'Papa had a wonderful library at home—' Ellie said.

But she broke off, conscious that she had said what she should not have, for her father's face was stiffening at the mention of all that he had lost.

She felt her expression tighten. They should not have come here. From the moment of their arrival she had been conscious of it. Leon was clearly steeling himself, and as for herself...

She glanced up at the château. Her father's home in exile. Thanks to Leon. *Only* thanks to Leon.

She felt her stomach knotting. Without Leon her father and his family would be homeless, penniless.

He's paying for all this—paying for all of them!

Just as he'd agreed he would when she'd agreed to marry him...

She'd known it—of course she had—but somehow being here, seeing her father and stepmother here, living at Leon's expense, settled here for the rest of their lives on his largesse, made her...uncomfortable. Ultra-conscious of the reasons behind her marriage. To give her father a secure home in exile—to give Leon a princess bride.

It was what their marriage had always been about—yet somehow, in the dizzying rush of passion and desire for Leon that had consumed her since their honeymoon, it had been so easy to forget it…so temptingly easy to forget the blunt truth of her marriage.

My title for his wealth.

A heaviness filled her, weighing her down. She heard Leon's voice in her memory, when they'd discussed their wedding preparations.

'Do you intend always to be this blunt about our marriage?' he had demanded.

And her answer—*'It's a pretty blunt situation.'*

But in the months since then, even though she'd felt the heaviness press at her again, she had done her best to forget that. Ignore it.

Deny it.

Deny it because she *wanted* to deny it! Had wanted to deny it, she knew now, with bitter self-awareness, ever since Leon had swept her off to his bed…

Because the bluntness of the truth about their marriage did not sit well with the bliss she had found in Leon's arms. It made a mockery of it.

A shout from the gardens below the terrace pierced her sudden bleakness.

'Lisi! You're here! Brilliant!'

A moment later her brother vaulted over the balustrade, his tennis racket clattering on to the stone terrace. Then he was wrapping her in an exuberant bear hug before clapping Leon on the back.

'Great to see you both!' he exclaimed, grabbing a

glass of orange juice and knocking it back as Marika made a more sedate entrance than her brother, coming up to hug Ellie.

The arrival of her half-siblings was a welcome release from the disquieting thoughts gripping her in such unwelcome fashion. But when Marika exclaimed expressively, her eyes speaking volumes, 'I'm *so* glad you're here!' Ellie had a different reason for disquiet.

There was a febrile quality to her sister she had not seen before—an air of suppressed excitement...of secretiveness...

But then Niki was targeting Leon, enthusiastically grilling him on the performance characteristics of his car, blatantly asking to take it out for a spin, promising—with a laugh—not to crash it. His exuberance lightened the atmosphere, and Ellie was glad. Gladder, too, when Niki turned to her.

'I need to celebrate!' He grinned insouciantly. 'I got my exam results through today, Lisi...'

Ellie's face lit and she was immediately diverted from the bleak thoughts in her head, grateful to be so. 'Oh, Niki—did you make your Oxford offer?'

He tilted his glass at her. 'Indeed I did,' he said.

'That's *wonderful*!' she exclaimed. 'Congratulations!' She turned to Leon. 'Niki's the brains in this family,' she said fondly.

'What are you going to be reading?' Leon asked.

And Ellie knew that, despite wishing he was not here, it was impossible for Leon to dislike her brother—his cheerful exuberance was a world away from the Grand Duke's chill formality.

'PPE,' he answered. 'Politics, Philosophy and Economics. Though it's the first and the last I'll be most focussed on. I'll need to be if I'm to—'

He broke off, his expression changing. He looked Leon in the eye.

'It's you I have to thank, and I am fully aware of it.' Suddenly he wasn't an exuberant teenager any more, but serious-faced, older than his years. 'The international student fees at Oxford are sky-high, and there's no way I could take up my place without your generosity.'

Ellie could see her father's expression stiffen at his son's blunt reminder of their dependence on his daughter's husband, and she felt herself stiffen, too. But Leon was simply nodding, telling Niki he could thank him by getting a first.

It was thanks to Niki that the evening was not the ordeal it would have been otherwise. His good-humoured remarks lightened the stolid conversation conducted by her father and stepmother, which centred mostly on the history of the château. Even so, it was heavy going, with Leon visibly unrelaxed, and Marika still with that distracted, febrile look about her.

Ellie was filled with unease. Her sister's parents seemed oblivious to it—but not Niki. From time to time Ellie distinctly saw him glancing at her…almost conspiratorially. She frowned inwardly. Something was going on, and she wasn't sure what. Antal, she assumed, with another silent sigh.

Her heart went out to her sister, pitying her. To love so hopelessly…how agonising must that be…?

She pulled her thoughts away. She had her own issues to deal with. She was wishing she had not come here. Yet knew it was good that she had.

No, not good—necessary.

Her face set. Yes, necessary to remind herself of just what her marriage was based on. Uncomfortable truth though it was. And it was time—more than time—that she acknowledged it…and not just to herself.

The long evening finally ended and, having drunk a dutiful *demi-tasse* of coffee from delicately translucent Sevres porcelain, in the exquisitely redecorated drawing room—all paid for by Leon—Ellie glanced at the antique ormolu clock on the marble mantelpiece—also paid for by Leon.

Marika and Niki had retired to a distant sofa and were absorbed in their phones—paid for by Leon— every now and then showing each other something on the screens, but saying nothing, which added to her unease.

Finally she felt she could get to her feet and bid her father and stepmother goodnight. Leon immediately did likewise, with barely disguised impatience, and she felt her face set again.

As they gained their apartments—just as beautifully decorated as the rest of the château, and all paid for by Leon—she turned to him.

'Leon, I'm sorry I dragged you here—but thank you for bringing me.' She swallowed, knowing she had to say this, to acknowledge it openly. 'And thank you… thank you for making all this possible.' Her arm swept around, encompassing the château and all that went with it. She took a breath, looking him square in the eyes, 'I am extremely appreciative of it.'

He was looking at her, a strange expression on his face. Frowning slightly.

'What's brought this on?' he posed.

Ellie's chin lifted. 'Just being here, Leon. Seeing it all for myself. What…what you've done for my family.' She swallowed again. 'And I'm glad Niki thanked you, too, for paying his uni fees.'

Leon started to shrug off his dinner jacket. 'He's OK, your brother. Unlike—' He stopped.

Ellie bit her lip, but tacitly acknowledged what Leon had not said. The ex-Grand Duke might be taking his luxurious exile for granted, but at least his son was aware of it.

'Niki is so different from my father,' she said awkwardly. 'He has a much more open nature—like our grandfather, Grand Duke Nikolai.' Her expression changed. 'I think it will help him, you know, now that he has to make his own way in the world and will be forced to make a future for himself outside Karylya, having had his life smashed to pieces. Everything he thought was stable has gone. The future he took for granted has simply…disappeared.'

She saw Leon's face tighten. Too late she remembered what he had said about his own youth—how the safe, secure world he'd grown up in had been ripped from him in the cataclysm of Greece's economic collapse. And how his father had abandoned him…

Hurriedly, she went on, sounding awkward again. 'I'm sorry. I didn't mean to compare my brother's situation to yours—you were younger, even!—and I am truly, truly grateful to you for making it possible for him to go to Oxford. I'm incredibly grateful for *everything*, Leon—everything you're doing for my family!'

His expression changed, softened. He disposed of

his jacket, walked up to her. He placed his hands on her shoulders. Warm through the thin silk of her gown. Holding her there.

'Stop,' he said. 'You don't have to say it. You don't have to thank me. It was what we agreed. Your father and his family get financial security and in exchange I...' his hands moulded her shoulders in a sensual gesture...possessive '...I get my princess bride.' His eyelids drooped. 'My incredibly beautiful, desirable, alluring and irresistible princess bride...'

With each word his voice grew more husky, his gaze washing over her.

'My irresistible princess bride,' he said again, his voice more husky still, 'whom I don't intend to resist a single moment longer after the most tediously long evening ever.'

Leon slid his hands languorously from her shoulders down her arms, to move around her pliant waist and draw her against him. He didn't like to see that troubled look in her eyes. He wanted to banish it. Banish it the swiftest way possible. The way he liked best—

He brushed Ellie's soft mouth with his, feeling his mood improve even as his desire quickened. His kiss deepened.

This—*this* was what he wanted! Ellie in his arms— his princess bride.

With effortless ease he swept her up to him, carrying her towards their waiting bed...

'Niki?'

Ellie's voice was tentative, but she knew she needed

to speak to him before she and Leon left the château that morning, and she was glad to find him on his own.

'Mmm?'

Her brother did not look up from his phone and she realised he was looking at a Karylyan newsfeed. She frowned. She was aware that the much-vaunted presidential elections that the council which had ousted her father had promised the population were fast approaching, but she had done her best not to pay attention to it. What point would there be? No one was going to vote to recall her father. Karylya would become a republic, with a president and not a grand duke, and that would be that.

She sighed, before saying as much to her brother. 'Niki, it will only upset you to follow the elections. They don't want us back and that's all there is to it. History has moved on. We have to accept it.' She paused. '*You* have to accept it.'

Her brother's face closed. 'Of course I accept it,' he said, his voice offhand. He gave a nonchalant, teenage-style shrug. 'Morbid curiosity, that's all.'

He tossed his phone on to the cushion of the chair he'd been sitting in and got to his feet. His expression lightened.

'So, sis, how's it all going with you and Leon? The celebrity rags are *full* of you! Is that what you intend to do with the rest of your life now? Non-stop jollies? Wall-to-wall parties?'

His words were light-hearted, but Ellie coloured.

'It's what Leon wants,' she said. She looked her brother square in the face. 'And, considering everything he's doing for our family, Niki, it's the least I can do!'

Niki sighed. 'If you put it that way…' he allowed.

Ellie's face tightened. What other way *could* it be put? Coming here to the château, seeing the reality of her father's situation, had made it impossible to hide from that.

Hadn't Leon spelt it out to her last night, before sweeping her up into his arms? Spelt it out as bluntly as she once had. He wanted a princess bride to show off—she wanted financial security for her penniless father.

Oh, Leon might tell her that he would never have married her without desiring her—or her desiring him—but that didn't take away the blunt underlying reason for their marriage.

He wouldn't have married me if I weren't a princess.

And she—she felt a hollowing inside her—she would not have married him had he not been rich enough to support her father and his family.

Her eyes shadowed. Before her marriage she had talked to her mother about her obligations and responsibilities as the princess she was—Princess Elizsaveta of Karylya—and she was still bound by them. Would always be bound by them. Whatever they cost her…

More than I dare allow.

Restlessly, she moved about the room, forcing aside her darkening thoughts. She could not pay them attention now. There would be time enough later… For now—right now—she had to seize this brief opportunity to speak to her brother about their sister. It would not easily come again.

'Niki, I'm worried about Marika,' she said roundly. 'Can't you help me convince her that she has to give up on Antal Horvath? Nothing can come of it! You know that as well as I do!'

Abruptly, her brother's expression changed. 'She'll be OK,' he said impatiently. 'Don't stress out over it!'

Ellie frowned. That had sounded like a typical off-hand remark any teenager might make, but she had heard an evasive note in it.

'Is she still in touch with him?' she pursued.

She saw that evasive blankness come over Niki's face again.

'How should I know?' He shrugged. He reached for his phone again, obviously wanting this interrogation to cease.

Ellie opened her mouth to challenge him, but her stepmother was coming into the room.

'Your father tells me you are leaving after lunch!' she announced, displeasure in her voice. 'This has been far too brief a visit, Elizsaveta!'

Ellie was apologetic—what else could she be?—and made mention of the social engagement she and Leon were committed to in Paris.

'Well, next time you must arrange to stay longer.' The Grand Duchess's tone was reprimanding. 'You have responsibilities to your father—do not forget that. You cannot spend your life perpetually flitting from one party to another!'

Ellie tensed. The fact that her stepmother had echoed her brother's criticism galled her. But she said nothing. For her father and stepmother, as for all the world, her marriage to Leon was a *coup de foudre* romance—how could she hurt them by slamming home the un-varnished truth?

But that unvarnished truth—the truth that she had become so dangerously neglectful of in the blissful weeks and months she'd spent with Leon—was something she must never let herself forget again.

She sighed inwardly as they drove off from the château later that day—Leon with a palpable air of relief—heading for that glittering social event in Paris where, yet again, she would arrive *en grande tenue*: Princess Elizsaveta of Karylya, dazzling Parisian high society with her beauty, her couture gown and the priceless jewels bestowed upon her by her impossibly handsome billionaire husband.

They would resume the endless social whirl he loved to enjoy with her at his side and she knew, with a sudden clenching of that emotion she would not name, that in such a marriage as theirs there could only be what they already had.

Friendship and desire.

What else could be between them?

However much she might long for there to be more—much, much more…

CHAPTER TWELVE

'WELL, I THINK that went off all right, don't you?'

There was a satisfied note in Leon's voice as he spoke, dropping his cufflinks on the vanity unit in their penthouse suite at the Viscari Roma, with its sweeping views over the ancient city.

'It was certainly a good turnout,' Ellie agreed, making her voice equable as she disengaged herself from her emerald necklace.

She felt a combination of being exhausted and strung-out. But she didn't want to let it show—it would spoil Leon's ebullient good mood.

They had hosted a party that evening, to repay all the invitations they had accepted since their wedding. It had been held in the hotel's banqueting suite—a glittering, opulent affair, no expense spared, that Ellie had thrown herself into organising with a determination that had been almost a frenzy, as if she were proving something to herself, to Leon. She had spared no effort to make it as dazzlingly brilliant as he could want and they themselves had been at the heart of it—Leon Dukaris, billionaire, and Princess Elizsaveta of Karylya, his royal bride, adorned in yet another priceless gown and draped with yet more priceless jewels.

As they'd received their guests, memory had plucked at her—their spectacular betrothal ball, where Leon had first kissed her...

How far I have come since then!

To a destination she had never dreamt of.

I never imagined it was waiting for me...

She felt emotion twist within her, but silenced it. She must always silence it.

Her eyes went to Leon now. He was looking as impossibly handsome as he always did, loosening his tie and chucking it aside to slip the top button of his dress shirt. She felt her breath catch—as it always did—felt that emotion she would not admit twist within her and crushed it back, as she always must.

He started to remove the diamond studs on his shirt, adding them to the gold cufflinks.

'Yes, definitely a good bag. A dozen royals, three *principessas* at least, one archduke, a couple of marquesses and I lost count of the counts!' he joshed.

Was it crass of him to take satisfaction in just how many of Europe's royal and aristocratic elite had attended the glittering party that had finally drawn to a close as dawn approached over the seven hills of Rome? After all, it was a long, long time since he'd stood in that line for the soup kitchen...

Do I really need to prove to myself—let alone the world—how far I've come since then? Prove that I will never go back to that misery again?

He was in a good place now—a very good place.

His eyes rested on Ellie, removing the emerald drops from her delicate earlobes—his beautiful, very own princess bride!—and they warmed as they always did.

Memory came to him of what he'd said to her so laconically that lunchtime so long ago now, when she had come to find out whether he really intended to marry her. How he'd told her that 'any princess' would do for him for a royal bride. Even her sister.

How absurd the idea seemed now!

No other princess could compare with Ellie.

No other *woman* could compare.

The words were in his head before he realised it, and hung there like an echo.

No other woman? Was *that* how he felt about Ellie?

His eyes fastened on her. She was lifting her hands now, to remove her tiara and unpin the ornate hairdo created by one of the top stylists in Rome to go with her exquisite couture gown in layers of pale green ombre silk.

No other woman...

The words were still there, resonating in his consciousness. Demanding he pay attention to them. Take in their meaning.

But Ellie's lustrous golden tresses were cascading down over her bare shoulders, distracting him from any thought but one.

He closed the distance between them. 'I believe,' he murmured, in a voice that was husky, 'you will need some help with the hooks of your gown...'

It was an office he was only too ready to perform for her. And all that came after...

Urgency filled him—urgency, desire and an arousal

so fierce he could only do what every instinct in his being impelled him to do. Yield to it.

But afterwards…long afterwards…Leon lay, his arms wrapped tight around her, their exhausted limbs still meshed, their hectic pulses slowly easing, yet again those words came to him that had entered his head unbidden…

No other woman.

Only Ellie. *His* Ellie. As he said her name in his head he felt once more—just as he had when she'd gazed up at him after their first incredible night together on their honeymoon—the strange sensation that something was thawing, deep inside him. What it was, he did not know—could not tell.

He would think about it later…

Right now the only priority was sleep—with this wondrous woman held tight in his possessing embrace. All that he wanted.

And in his arms—his in exchange for the security she sought for her father, her body sated with the passion of their union—she stared with sleepless eyes into the dark room, knowing with the clutching of emotion in her that was like a pain, that what she had now was all that she could ever have…

Ellie was sitting on the sofa in the sitting room of their suite at the Viscari, methodically working her way through the latest batch of gilt-edged invitations that had flooded in after their own lavish party, dutifully checking with Leon which ones to accept.

He gave a careless shrug, walking back to her from

where he'd been standing by the doors opening on to their balcony, looking out over the roofs of Rome with a slight frown on his brow, hands thrust into his trouser pockets.

'Say no to all of them if you like,' he said. His expression changed. 'You know,' he mused, 'maybe we should call time on all this socialising. Maybe,' he said, 'after that mega-bash of our own, we'd like a break from it.'

Ellie looked across at him, her expression flickering. 'Only if you want to,' she said uncertainly.

He quirked an eyebrow. 'And what do *you* want?' he countered.

'I want to do what *you* want,' she answered.

It was the answer she would always give…must always give. And she must be scrupulous in doing so.

I can't forget—must not forget!—the reasons we are married.

Since their return from the château it had been her mantra. Diligently repeated to herself.

Leon frowned. 'That's not an answer,' he said.

Ellie bit her lip. 'What…what answer would you like from me, Leon?'

His expression darkened. 'Don't talk like that!' His frown deepened. 'Ellie, what's up?' He skewered her with his dark eyes.

She swallowed. 'Nothing—' she began.

His mouth tightened. 'Yes, there is.' He eyed her narrowly. 'Something's wrong, Ellie. Don't tell me otherwise. Ever since…' He paused, his mouth tightening again. 'Ever since we came back from visiting your father!'

He took a breath.

'Do you think I haven't noticed the difference in you? You got stuck into organising our party like there was no tomorrow and you haven't relaxed since. Something's eating you. At first I put it down to you being…well, upset…whatever…seeing your father again now that he's exiled and so on. And then…' He frowned again. 'And then while we were there you trotted out all that stuff about being grateful to me for paying for the damn château, for paying your brother's university fees—'

He stopped. Eyeballed her. This was important and he wanted it clear.

'You do *not*,' he said, 'have to thank me—*ever*!' His expression changed, and there was a rueful humour in it now. 'You were the one who spelt it out to me, remember? Set out just what the conditions were for your agreeing to marry me! So no thanks are due in either direction.'

She was looking at him, with an expression on her face he hadn't seen before. Heavy and tense. He didn't like to see it there.

'No, but there are obligations, Leon—and that is what I am fully aware of.' Her voice was sombre, serious. Unflinching. 'You've provided for my father and my reciprocal obligation is to be, and do, what *you* want. You wanted a princess bride, and that…' she took a breath '…that is what I am. Your princess bride. And *you* get to choose where and when and how often to show me off—I don't.'

As she spoke, Ellie saw his face darken again. For a second a frisson of apprehension went through her, but she held her ground. Inside, she was conscious of a silent cry—but she must give no voice to it. She had silenced it for weeks now—ever since they'd driven away from the château.

Silenced it to him.

Silenced it to herself.

A word broke from him. Coarse, she could tell—but it was in Greek, and she was thankful not to understand it.

Tension racked through her suddenly. Had she been tactless, spelling it out like that? But that was what she'd done at that restaurant before their wedding, insisting on a bluntness about the reasons for their marriage that she would not try to disguise. Not then—and not now. Not any more.

I almost made myself forget—because I wanted to forget! Because I was so swept away by him!

Swept away to a place she had never thought to go with him—a destination that had never been part of her reason for marrying him!

But it was a place she must not approach again.

I have to keep to the limits of our marriage. Anything else is...

Impossible.

The bleak word hung in the echo of his expletive.

She saw him take a breath. Saw something flash in his eyes like gold.

'To hell with showing you off! And to hell,' he said, 'with you being a princess! I want *you*, Ellie! *You!* The beautiful, irresistible *you*! *You* are the woman I want!'

He reached forward, hauled her to her feet, planted his hands on her hips and held her right in front of him.

'I couldn't care less about bankrolling your father— if it gets me *you*!'

He took another ragged breath, and another flash of gold seared across his eyes.

'So, do you get that?'

The expression in his flashing eyes softened. His hands lifted to her face, cupping her cheeks with a tenderness in his touch.

'Do you get it?' he asked again, and now his voice was thickening, the gold in his eyes turning molten. 'Because if you don't…' he said, and now there was a huskiness in his voice that was melting through her, making her limbs suddenly weak even as she felt as light as air, as if she were being lifted up with every word he said. 'If you don't I'm just going to have to kiss you senseless until you *do* get it…'

He lowered his mouth to hers. To Ellie—the woman he wanted…the woman no other could compare with.

His kiss was slow and lingering. The revelation that had come on him in the night possessed him— that there was no other woman for him but Ellie…his Ellie…princess or no princess. He couldn't care less… not any more.

He lifted his mouth away. There was a dazed look in her eyes and he smiled, well pleased.

'Let's get out of here,' he said. 'Out of the city— away from everyone! Get into the car and drive…' His eyes caressed her. 'I want you all to myself—I'm done with showing off to everyone. Let's head to where no one knows us. I want…' his voice grew husky, his eyes washing over her '…a second honeymoon…'

He saw her face light up—knew he had said exactly the right thing. He let her ago. If he kissed her again he knew they'd just end up back in bed, and he was filled now with a sudden impatience. He wanted to get out of Rome.

'Where shall we go?' he asked. 'Somewhere deserted that we can drive to—somewhere by the sea—it's too hot for anything else!—but not too far away. I want to get there today!'

'I don't think anywhere is completely deserted in Italy in the summer...' Ellie answered faintly.

Emotions were sweeping through her, lifting her off her feet. All the heaviness that had crushed her since visiting her father had evaporated. In its place a new emotion was soaring. One she dared not even name.

But for all that she knew what it was—and why.

Hope.

How could it be anything else, with Leon wanting to sweep her off on a second honeymoon...?

Oh, what if it's really true, what he is telling me? That he wants me—the woman I am! Not the Princess! Oh, if that's really, really true—

She broke off her thoughts, not daring to go further. Instead, gathering her soaring hopes, she pulled them into a semblance of sense.

'Um...maybe Puglia?' she ventured. 'Not as touristy as places like Amalfi or Portofino. And Puglia,' she added, with a sudden eagerness in her voice, 'has *trulli*! Oh, Leon, can we stay in a *trullo*? Please say we can!'

Her spirits were soaring still.

* * *

Leon laughed indulgently. 'We shall stay anywhere you like!' he promised expansively.

He'd said the right thing to her—said the right thing to himself! What did he care if the woman standing there in front of him, her eyes shining like stars, had a drop of royal blood in her?

Not a jot or an iota.

Then, abruptly, he frowned. 'What are *trulli*?' he demanded.

His answer was a laugh. 'Traditional stone houses in Puglia—they're round, with very pointy tiled cone-shaped roofs, and they are absolutely *adorable*!' Ellie exclaimed happily.

'Let's go for it,' Leon said decisively. 'We'll leave our fancy togs here and head off. Right now!'

Ellie needed no urging and whisked into the bedroom to start packing, her feet still not touching the floor.

Their *trulli*—for the secluded villa consisted of a linked cluster of several of the beautifully restored conical buildings, set in the grounds of a converted *masseria* farmstead—proved every bit as adorable as Ellie wanted. And their holiday in Puglia was as blissful as she could ever have dreamt. A second honeymoon indeed.

Leon had swapped his monster car for a far more practical and less eye-catching SUV, and in it they explored the ancient towns of Puglia, with their ornate basilicas and crumbling buildings, their air of sleepy isolation from the busy world in the somnolent heat of high summer.

There were tourists, true, but it still felt uncrowded, and she and Leon blended easily with them, both of them dressed down in shorts and T-shirts, with Ellie wearing nothing more fancy in the evenings than a floaty cotton skirt and lacy top—perfectly fine for eating out at harbourside *trattoria*, or cooking for themselves at their villa—simple pasta dishes or barbecued steak, grilled fish, freshly caught, anything that was easy—and drinking the local wines.

It was a universe away from their glitzy life as Leon the billionaire showing off his royal bride to the admiring world and Princess Elizsaveta of Karylya.

As the days passed in a leisurely parade they set no particular end-point to their sojourn here. Their meandering days sometimes took them inland, to discover almost deserted villages lapped by endless olive groves, sometimes down to the coast to swim off the rocks in the crystal-clear waters of the Adriatic, and they even ventured to Lecce, the Florence of the South, to admire its baroque extravagance—*barocco lecchese*, as she informed Leon from the guidebook as they strolled around the *centro storico*, the historic heart of the city.

Ellie knew she had never been happier in her life.

And knew why.

She had Leon all to herself! Just as she had yearned to have that night that seemed so long ago now, above the marina in Monte Carlo, with the sound of fashionable revelry coming up from the lavish yachts. That was something she missed not at all, she knew with absolute certainty. Nor all it stood for.

And nor, it seemed, did Leon.

After abandoning any plans for an expedition that day, content to enjoy their *trulli*'s charms, they were lying by their pool, shaded from the hot sun by a parasol, and he stroked her thigh idly to get her attention as she drowsed beside him, sleepy after their *al fresco* lunch of fresh-baked bread with cheese, dried meats and ripe tomatoes, drenched in olive oil from the groves nearby, with luscious peaches for dessert, washed down by the Puglian white wine Verdeca.

'When we leave here shall we change our ways?' he asked.

She looked across at him. There was something new in his voice—something she had not heard before.

'I told you in Rome I was done with non-stop socialising. I've had my fill of it—for good.'

Leon spoke decisively, knowing he meant what he'd just said. OK, so he'd got a massive kick out of it originally, revelling in having the world see him walk into a room with not just a royal bride, but the most breathtaking royal bride there had ever been! But, hey, he'd been there now—done that and got the T-shirt.

His expression tightened momentarily. And besides, there was no way he ever wanted Ellie saying to him again what she had said to him that morning in Rome. That she felt she had some kind of obligation to do whatever it was he wanted.

He pushed the memory aside roughly.

I don't want that having anything to do with our marriage! We've gone beyond that. Way beyond.

He turned his head to look at her, seeing her eyes

on him, a question in them. A question he was going to answer.

His hand dropped from her thigh to pick up hers. He meshed his strong fingers with her delicate slender ones and raised it to his mouth, kissing it with something that was not homage or desire…

It was affection.

He felt something warm within him—that strange sense of thawing that he had felt before and didn't understand. But knew it was good to feel it, whatever it was.

He folded her hand in his and dropped it to his bared chest, taking a breath. This was important and he wanted to get it right.

Just as I had to get it right on our honeymoon, when I realised how much was at stake.

Just as much was at stake now.

Maybe more.

The thought was in his head and he held it there, seeking the words he needed to say.

'Ellie, I know we married to achieve our own particular aims—your title for my wealth, just as you've always said. But…' He paused, taking another breath, unable to read her expression, only knowing that there was an absolute stillness about her suddenly. 'We've achieved those aims, haven't we? Your father and his family are safely settled, and I…' He gave a rueful laugh. 'Well, I've showed you off to the entire world as my princess bride!'

His expression changed, and he felt the constraint in it suddenly.

'That soup kitchen in Athens was a long time ago and

I can let it go now. I've nothing to prove to the world. Not any more.'

He saw something move in her eyes and knew it for what it was—compassion. But she said nothing, only perhaps tightened her fingers on his. He felt his throat constrict suddenly, as if that look of compassion were too much for him—as if he had to keep it out, away from him.

Because if he didn't—

He felt his muscles clench suddenly and knew he was fighting for control—a control it was absolutely essential he retained. As he had always done—had had to—all his adult life.

Even before his adult life.

No! He would not go there. He was not revisiting the past—he was escaping it!

He made himself breathe out slowly before speaking again. Knowing he must get it right.

'Ellie, what we have together is *good.* Both in bed and out! And…and we're happy together, aren't we? So…' He took another breath and then he said it. 'So why don't we just be ourselves? You and me—just… well, *us.*'

She wasn't saying anything, and he could feel the tension mounting in him. Had he got it wrong? He'd got it wrong on their wedding night—read her wrong and nearly lost what he'd wanted so much.

'Ellie—say something…'

His hand tightened on hers as if he would not let her go. *Could* not let her go.

'Say we have a chance, at least a chance, of making

ours a real marriage! Nothing to do with me being rich and you being royal! And not bound by any time limit.'

He took another breath, his eyes fixed on her, willing her to say something…anything…

Anything but no.

'What do you say?' he prompted.

He had to know—he *had* to!

There was a knot inside him and it was pulling tighter. He saw her face working, saw something in her eyes he could not read. And then she moistened her lips, as if they'd gone suddenly dry, and he heard her speak.

'I say yes,' she said.

For a moment there was silence, and then, a torrent of Greek breaking from him, he drew her bodily across him, hauling her to his chest.

His eyes burned gold, bright as the sun. 'This,' he said, and his voice was husky, 'calls for a celebration.'

He meshed his fingers in her golden hair, his mouth seeking hers, filled with an emotion he could not name. He only knew that it was good. It was very, *very* good…

CHAPTER THIRTEEN

'WE'RE GOING TO need a place of our own to live. We can't live out of hotels any longer.'

Leon's voice was decisive as he gazed around their suite at the Viscari Roma. The city had seemed noisy and crowded since their return from Puglia, and he wanted out. Wanted to be done with hotel living altogether.

'So, where do you fancy?' he asked. 'The world is our oyster!'

OK, so privately he hoped she wouldn't say *A château on the Loire next to my father*, but if that really was what she wanted he'd go along with it.

Hell, he'd go along with anything she wanted.

His gaze softened. How right he'd been to put it to the test that afternoon—to risk all and claim not his princess bride but his wife.

My wife.

His eyes swept over her. They were dining in their suite, neither of them wanting to go out or to face the hotel restaurant.

My wife.

He said it again to himself, hearing the words in his head.

Certainty was filling him—this was the woman he wanted to be with. Not because of her royal blood—and not even because of her extraordinary beauty. He knew that with a strange realisation. It was for more than that—much more.

And he knew with equal certainty that he wanted it for much longer than the mere two years she'd stipulated when they'd hammered out their marriage terms all those months ago.

Everything's changed since then!

Everything had changed and it was so much better than he had ever dreamt it could be.

'We don't just have to have just one place, of course,' he said now. 'We can have homes all over!' He gave a laugh. 'Let's pick a country we both like and start there. How about it?'

He was keen to get going on house-hunting. He wanted to make a home with Ellie. A home *life* with her.

He saw there was a considering look on Ellie's face.

'Would it seem very tame to pick England?' ventured Ellie. 'It's what I'm most used to. Now that Karylya—'

She stopped. No point stating the obvious. And definitely no point thinking of anything sad at all.

Not when happiness was soaring through her. Had been soaring through her ever since Leon had, in this very room, told her that he didn't care if she were royal or not. And then on that day in Puglia, lying by the pool at their enchanting *trulli*, he had said what she knew she had longed to hear.

I wanted more—oh, much more than what we had! So much more! But I didn't dare say it—didn't dare think it.

But now—oh, now she dared. Dared to do more still.

Now, finally, I dare to admit what I feel for him! Not just friendship—not just desire. But love.

Wonder filled her. She had married him out of duty and yet love had been waiting for her all along!

As she gazed at him, her heart full, she veiled her eyes lest her love blaze out too brightly. She must take this gently—the revelation was still too new, too fresh.

Leon had said no word of love to her—but if *she* had only just realised the depths of her feelings for him she must allow that he, like her, might not yet think in those terms.

But surely he would one day? Surely she had every reason to hope that he would move to that same glorious realisation?

He has said he wants ours to be a real marriage— and what else is a real marriage but one based on love?

He needed time, that was all—she was sure of it. Time to discover, as she had done, just how deeply he felt about her. And she would be waiting for him when he did so—when he gave his love to her and she gave him hers.

A glow set about her, radiating her happiness.

'Not tame at all,' Leon was saying.

She brought her mind back to the subject in question, away from that golden image in her imagination of Leon clasping her to him and saying how infinitely he loved her!

'So, whereabouts in England should we start looking?' he went on. 'Your mother and stepfather live in Somerset—is that right? Would that be a good place to look first? All I know about it is that it's famous for cider. We could have a cider orchard of our own.'

Settling near Lady Connie and her bluff husband would be no problem for him, he mused. As for the ex-Grand Duke—well, he was welcome to sponge off him for the rest of his life with his compliments. It was of no account to him.

Only Ellie mattered. His wonderful, wonderful wife Ellie—with whom he was going to spend the rest of his life and be happy every single day of it! Nothing could stop that now.

Because our marriage is based on what is honest and true—not on deceit and delusion. So it will stand the test of time. Stand all tests.

'Somerset's beautiful!' Ellie replied enthusiastically.

Thinking of her mother made her long to visit her as soon as possible. To tell her how groundless her fears had proved—how much she loved the man she'd married for duty…

She felt her heart glow with warmth.

'Good,' Leon was saying in his decisive fashion, and they fell to discussing what kind of property they might like to live in.

'We'll need somewhere warmer for winter breaks, though,' he went on. 'How about a villa in the Caribbean? We'll explore the islands and pick the one we like best.'

Enthusiasm fired him. How right he'd been to want so much more from this marriage of theirs! His wonderful wife Ellie, their companionship together, the searing desire that flamed between them... And now to settle down together, make their lives together.

What better could there possibly be?

Gladness filled him.

I have everything I want—everything! I want for nothing more—nothing at all.

The next week passed in a happy blur. Because they did not wish to be uncivil, there were still some outstanding invitations they felt they should honour. But they were already in touch with estate agents, and had a list of potential properties to view the following week, when they would visit Ellie's mother on her return to the UK.

They had also agreed that Ellie would stop by her father en route to England, to tell him in person of their plans to settle in the UK, while Leon flew on to London to check up on his business affairs. Besides, the presidential elections were imminent in Karylya, and she wanted to support her father at such an inevitably upsetting time.

Her brother was due to go up to Oxford at the end of the month, to start his degree. He was visiting some school friends in Switzerland, and she hoped it would distract him from the news in Karylya.

As for Marika... Ellie sighed as she sent her a lengthy text, making it as cheerful as she could. Her mood would be particularly down at the prospect of Antal's father becoming President, setting the final seal on the impossibility of her sister ever finding her longed-for happy-ever-after with Antal.

A wave of pity for her sister swept through her. Loving without hope. How heartbreaking that must be, compared with her own wonderful, radiant happiness.

Her eyes glowed with it every time she looked at Leon, met his glance at her. She felt her hopes soar. Oh, surely soon Leon would realise he felt for her what she felt for him? Surely her hopes would be fulfilled! It was just a matter of time, that was all…

And until then she would wait patiently, loyally, bathing in the happiness she had, and in the wonderful future she was looking forward to. Making a home with Leon. Being his loving wife for ever!

How happy I am! How absolutely happy!

The thought ran in Ellie's head constantly, like a silent companion. Nothing could spoil it now—she was certain of it.

Ellie paused in packing her toiletries bag and glanced at her phone screen again, frowning. Anxiety nipped though she tried to dismiss it.

She and Leon were leaving Rome in the morning, by private jet. She would deplane at Angers, and Leon would fly on to London. She couldn't get to Angers soon enough. She wanted to see Marika…talk to her. Her assiduously encouraging text to her sister had brought a vehement response.

Lisi, you haven't the faintest idea! Not being with Antal is agony! Pure agony! I love him so, so much! I just want to be with him! I can't bear my life without him! And I'm not going to!

Ellie had texted back immediately, but there had been no further reply. She'd texted Niki, too—no reply from him either.

OK, so he was probably out, but she wanted him to phone Marika, make sure she was…

Was what?

She felt that stab of anxiety nip again. Marika had never sounded so openly fraught—or so despairing. She wanted to phone her, but she knew it would not go down well with Leon if she disappeared into the sitting room for half an hour of sisterly consolation, with Marika weeping over the ether.

She could see him from the en suite bathroom, lying on the bed in his bathrobe, idly flicking through printouts for the houses they were going to be viewing, a glass of cognac on his bedside table. She could see from his glances at her that he was impatient for her to be done with packing—and with texting. He had that look, that anticipatory gold-flecked glint in his eye that she knew well. And as they wouldn't be seeing each other for several days she wanted to make the most of tonight—just as he did.

She would try one final text. She didn't like the way Marika had ended her last one—she didn't like it at all. Extravagant hyperbole, probably, but all the same…

I can't bear my life without him! And I'm not going to!

* * *

'What's up?'

Leon tried to penetrate Ellie's clearly uneasy thoughts. He set aside the estate agents' print-outs he'd been whiling away the time with, reaching for his cognac, wanting Ellie to be done with fussing over her creams and cosmetics—she didn't need them to make her any more beautiful than she was.

His eyes washed over her slender form, enticingly outlined by her silk peignoir. Her lovely face was frowning as she tapped at her phone. He didn't want her texting and he didn't want her frowning—he wanted her to come to bed so he could make love to her...

'Marika's not answering my texts,' Ellie said, that frown still on her brow.

Leon reached for his cognac again, feeling irritated. Ellie's woebegone sister had always irritated him. 'Moping over her boyfriend, most like,' he said. 'As usual.'

Ellie bit her lip. 'She can't help being hopelessly in love—' she began.

Leon replaced his cognac glass with a sudden movement. He was more than fed up with the perpetually lovelorn Marika. Yet another example of how the pernicious delusion of love screwed up lives, ruined happiness...

'That's exactly what she *can* help!' he snapped. 'Your sister's a fool! Don't waste your sympathy on her—it won't help a thing!'

He jack-knifed to a sitting position.

'She needs to grow up—get real!'

* * *

Ellie stared—his voice had been so scathing.

She rushed to defend her sister. 'She *is* real, Leon! She's breaking her heart over Antal—'

A word broke from him.

Dimly, Ellie recognised it as the same Greek expletive he'd come out with when she'd said it was her obligation to let him show her off endlessly as his princess bride…

His face darkened. 'No,' he said, and there was an implacable note in his voice she had never heard before, as if what he said could never be gainsaid. 'She just imagines she is! Like I said, she needs to grow up! Grow up and learn that nobody breaks their heart—*nobody*! That nobody is *worth* breaking your heart over!'

'But that's just what I'm afraid of!'

The words came out in a rush. Whether it was her reaction to Leon's out-of-the-blue vehemence she didn't know, but suddenly she was coming towards him with her phone, its screen illuminated, all the anxiety she'd felt and had tried to suppress leaping in her.

'Look!' She held the phone out, then realised that the texts were all in Karylyan. 'It's what she says, Leon: I can't bear my life without him. And I'm not going to.'

In front of her eyes she saw his face masked, as if a steel visor had come down over it. He got to his feet, coming around the bed to her. There was a fury in his eyes that made her step back. But he reached for her shoulders, pinioning her with a hard, immovable grip.

Blackness was in him—a dark, bitter tide. It had come from nowhere, suddenly unleashed by Ellie's unthinking words, her maudlin sentiments about her idiotic sister who was moping in endless self-inflicted misery—totally unnecessary and indefensible self-inflicted misery! Wallowing in a fantasy that hadn't existed in the first place! Ruining her life because of it.

And not just her own life.

Memory slashed at him of another time—another woman—and he tore it from him. No, he would not go there. He refused to go there. He would stay only in this place he had made for himself. Facing reality square-on.

'If you seriously believe that then phone your father, your stepmother, right now. Tell them to go and check on her!' he ground out. 'Otherwise listen to me—*listen* to me.'

He took a breath, a searing breath that razored his lungs. The darkness was still inside him, roiling in his vision. He had to make her see—*understand!* Understand the essential truth.

'I say your sister is a fool—and I mean it! A fool because she believes in something that doesn't exist! She only thinks it does—and look where that has got her? Where does it get anyone? It doesn't get them anywhere! It screws them up—that's all! Screws up lives, Ellie! Ruins them and destroys them! And all for something that doesn't even exist! Because it's garbage—all of it! All that hearts and flowers, all those vows and promises! Just garbage! Toxic garbage!'

Shock was naked in her face and it angered him. Angered him that she was shocked at what he was saying. He was telling her the truth.

The truth she has to believe—just as I do!

And she did believe it—of course she did! Why

would she have married him otherwise? If she'd been like her sister—obsessed by some poisonous fantasy, believing in it—she would never have married him!

He felt the black tide that had swept over him like a tsunami out of nowhere beginning to recede. The pressure of his hands on her shoulders slackened, but he did not let her go. She was staring at him, and he could see a pulse beating at her throat. He didn't want her upset. He needed to calm her—calm himself.

'Ellie, it's OK—it's OK.'

His hands moulded her shoulders. He wanted to take her in his arms, but there were things he needed to say first. To reassure her—reassure himself.

'Look, why do you think we're so good together? Why do you think our marriage works so well?' His voice had lost the last of its vehemence—but not its emphasis. 'Why do you think it's going to go on working all our lives together?'

He took a breath, feeling his thumping heart-rate easing now, thankful that the black tide had left him, receded back into the past he never wanted to let it out from again. His eyes were pouring into hers now, making her see, making her understand, spelling it out to her.

'Right from the start we avoided any of that hearts and flowers, vows and promises rubbish! We never pretended anything to each other! Oh, the press might have drooled that we were some kind of sentimental fairy-tale romance—it sells papers! But we've known better right from the off! We've never deceived ourselves about why we married! We were honest with each other and we're honest with each other still. Our marriage has moved on and we're taking it forward together. Clear-eyed and honest. Neither of us is fooling ourselves or trying to fool each other.'

He took another breath, knowing he never wanted to have this conversation again—that he wanted it done with for ever.

His hands pressed on her shoulders, warm and re-assuring. 'We both know that *love*—' he said the word with scathing, sarcastic inflection '—has got nothing to do with us! *That's* what makes our marriage so successful! Why it works so brilliantly! And it will go on working brilliantly! It's the same for every relationship that actually works—by keeping love well and truly out of it!'

He saw her swallow. The pulse at her throat was still beating strongly, but there was a pallor to her skin, a sharpening of her cheekbones.

Something shuttered in her eyes. 'Are you saying,' she asked slowly, 'that you don't think couples are ever in love with each other?'

Leon's lip curled. 'Oh, they may *think* they are,' he said derisively, 'but more fool them! Both of them are deluded! Thinking themselves in love makes an unholy mess of things! Because when the chips go down they'll find out for themselves, too late, how much garbage it all is!' There was an edge in the way he was speaking now, sharp and serrated. 'That all their hearts and flowers, their vows and promises, mean nothing—just empty words!'

A chill was starting to spread inside Ellie—as if icy water were being poured into her veins. She could feel her heart thudding in her chest. Too much emotion was in her, poured upon her out of nowhere, without any warning. And it seemed to be draining into a vortex that was sucking everything out of her. Everything that was her...

'What about...?' She swallowed. 'What about when *you* fall in love, Leon?'

She saw the same dark expression flash across his face that she had seen when she had read out Marika's despairing text. Before he had shocked her with his furious outburst...

'I never will,' he retorted harshly. 'I told you—it doesn't exist.' He held her distended gaze, his dark eyes implacable. 'It doesn't exist,' he said again. 'So I will *never* tell a woman I love her. Will *never* tell her that lie.'

Something twisted along the tight line of his mouth. His eyes were boring into hers.

'And I never want to hear a woman tell me she loves me—*never*. I don't want *any* woman to say she loves me—and certainly not you!' he finished emphatically.

Finally his voice softened, and his hands started to caress her shoulders, kneading them, trying to draw her to him, hold her in his arms.

'Because you are too important to me, Ellie.' His voice was husky now, and his eyelids started to droop over his eyes. 'Who needs illusions, or delusions, or dangerous fantasies, when we have what *we* have—so much better, so much more real...'

Leon lowered his mouth to hers, moving over it sensually, arousingly. Desire pooled in him—honest and true. As honest and true as everything else that there was between them. What there would always be down all their years together...

Somewhere...dimly...way beyond the quickening of his desire, the quickening of his body as he drew this wonderful, beautiful, irresistible woman into his arms—his bride, his wife, his own most precious treasure—he became aware of two things.

Her phone was ringing.

And she was not kissing him back.

CHAPTER FOURTEEN

ELLIE HEARD HER PHONE. As if she were a sleepwalker she pulled herself free, staring at the number. Everything seemed distorted, as if the whole world had suddenly tilted—warped.

She thought it must be Marika, finally phoning her back. Or Niki.

It was her father.

And as she realised that the world suddenly shifted into terrifying focus. Fear knifed through her.

She answered the phone. Heard her father's voice. Answered in Karylyan.

Then she disengaged and stared at Leon. Who was staring at her, waiting to be told.

'That was my father. Marika has gone—left for Switzerland. She's…she's going to Karylya. And Niki—' she swallowed '—is taking her there.'

For a moment she just stood there, as if paralysed. All that was in her head, just for a second, was relief at the fact that she'd totally misinterpreted what her sister had meant by her vehement text. The next second the relief had vanished.

If Marika and Niki reached Karylya…

Urgently, she swung round, swinging open the door of the wardrobe, where her outfit for the flight tomorrow was hanging. But she would not be flying to Angers now.

Thank God I'm ready to travel—my hand luggage, my handbag, both sorted. My passport...

Her passport most of all.

Essential.

She felt her forearm seized as she moved to take out her clothes.

'Ellie—stop. What the hell are you doing?' Leon's voice was urgent.

She stared at him. There was a tempest in her head, but she could not pay it any attention right now.

'I'm going after them.'

'*What?* Are you mad? Ellie, the moment they reach the border they'll either be stopped or arrested! They're banned from entering the country! And so are you!'

She shook herself free. 'Princess Elizsaveta of Karylya is—but my passport is British. Ellie Peters. I'm a British citizen. They can't touch me!'

He swore. Not in Greek this time, but in an Anglo-Saxon vernacular that she understood only too well. She ignored it—just as she ignored what he was saying now, his eyes flashing angrily.

'Of course they damn well can! They can do anything they like! Matyas Horvath is a political hard man who is turning Karylya into a police state, and he will be president by the end of the week! Of *course* he'll jail you! Jail the lot of you! All you and your moronically irresponsible siblings will achieve is to feed his propa-

ganda machine—he'll make huge political capital out of
it! You'll be playing right into his hands if you go there!'

Her face contorted. 'I don't care! Leon! I have to *try*!
I have to do *something*!'

'But *not* chase after them! I absolutely forbid it!'

She froze. Colour flared in her face.

'You can't stop me,' she said.

She said it coldly, deliberately. Biting out each word.

He took a step away from her, but still his height tow-
ered over hers. His face had hardened—just as it had
when she had told him about her sister's text.

Anguish speared her. Oh, dear God, fool that she had
been—unforgivable fool!

But she could not think about that now—could not
think about the tempest raging in her head. She could
only force her mind to do what it had to do now—make
her body do what it had to.

To go after her sister, her brother—

And Leon would not stop her. *Could* not stop her.

'No,' he said, and his voice was as heavy as lead, as
hard as iron, 'I can't stop you. But what I can do—and
I will, be very, very sure of that, if you insist on this
insanity—is pull the financial plug on your father. Totally. Right now.' He ground each word out, his features
frozen and rigid.

A gasp broke from her, ragged and torn.

Leon plunged on. He had to make her understand—
understand in what seemed to be the only way to penetrate the insane stupidity of what she was planning.

He felt emotions war within him. One was blinding
fury at what she was trying to do—walk into a country

that was days away from becoming a one-man dictatorship. But the other emotion was stronger still.

Gut-wrenching, convulsing fear.

Fear that he might lose her to years of incarceration—maybe for ever.

I can't lose her—I can't!

The horror of it leapt again. Making his voice harsh. Making him ruthless in preventing her madness by whatever means possible. He would exert the only leverage over her that he had. To keep her safe from herself. Safe for him.

Harsh lines incised around his mouth. 'If you go after them I will evict your father and his wife, render them penniless. I can do it—and I *will*, Ellie.'

The words seemed carved into the space between them.

She was staring at him, her face as white as a sheet. Her hands were clenching and unclenching at her sides, her breathing laboured. It was like a knife in his guts to see her like that, but he had to do it. Had to do it for her sake—for his.

Then, abruptly, she slumped, her hands falling limply slack. She looked at him with weary, stricken, defeated eyes.

'You win, Leon. I can't do that to my father—not now.'

She turned away, half stumbling. He moved to catch her, but she evaded him.

He spoke again, his voice clipped, decisive.

'I'll rearrange our flight to take you straight to your father's tonight. It's late, but doable.'

* * *

Ellie heard him speak through a mind numbed with too much shock—too much fear for her sister and her brother.

It stayed numb—blessedly numb—all the way to the airport, long past the midnight hour, where she was escorted by Leon on to the private jet, to have him kiss her cheek, then stride down the steps, back to the car waiting on the Tarmac, while the cabin door was swung shut, the plane starting to taxi.

In her head she heard Leon's last words to her on their way here—the assurances he'd tried to give her.

'I'll start kicking up all the hell I can—the Karylyan embassy in Rome, human rights lawyers, press, governments—whatever it takes, Ellie. Whatever it damn well takes to get them back!'

Only as the plane soared off into the night sky did the numbness leave her.

And in its place only two emotions were left to her.

Fear for her siblings.

Despair for herself.

At the château, when she arrived in the early hours of the morning, her father swept her up into his arms, holding her tightly. Even her stepmother embraced her. They both looked haggard, as did Ellie.

'Leon persuaded me that I would only make things worse if I followed Marika and Niki,' she told them, as they made a sketchy breakfast for which none of them had any appetite. 'I thought my British passport would protect me, but—'

'Horvath will respect *nothing*!' her father burst out.

'Is there any news from them?' her stepmother asked frantically.

Ellie could only shake her head. She'd been texting constantly, ever since landing, but no reply had come. She had no idea where Marika and Niki were—or what had happened to them. Her eyes went to the television set, tuned to the Karylyan news channel for the breakfast news—all it was showing was the preparations for the election, and the presenter was fulsomely extolling Matyas Horvath as the best candidate for president. The only candidate...

'The media dare say nothing else,' Ellie's father said grimly. 'The clampdown on press freedom has been comprehensive.'

Ellie fished out her tablet. 'There is *some* real news coming out,' she said cautiously. 'Pretty clandestine, but it's hard for Horvath to silence the Internet entirely.'

She found the unofficial newsfeed that she had been following all the way from Angers. It was being broadcast from outside Karylya, and there was some criticism about the elections having been manipulated—criticism over Horvath being the sole candidate. It lamented the fact that no other candidate was brave enough to stand against him, to be a rallying point for all those who opposed the looming dictatorship.

She checked her phone again. Still nothing from Marika or Niki. Fear clutched at her. Had they been stopped at the border—were they already in detention? No one would know until the new regime was ready to make propaganda out of it.

Her eyes went back to the TV screen, and then again to her tablet, her heart heavy and fearful...

The morning passed, the hours leaden, and still there was no news. No contact.

Leon phoned her briefly, sounding strained and terse, asking for any news, saying he would be in touch again later, telling her to keep him informed. Then he rang off.

Hearing his voice had been...difficult.

She could hear her father in the library, talking to one of his small staff, preparing a press statement to be issued if it was discovered that his children were intercepted. He asked only for their safe return, said that they were young and misguided—innocent of all except youthful folly.

Would it be enough to secure their safety? Or would Matyas Horvath make political capital out of it, as Leon had warned—even subject them to a trial of some kind, sentence them to prison...

The very thought of it sent knives into her stomach. She knew Leon had been right to castigate Niki and Marika for being so insanely reckless—for going now, at the worst of times, into the lion's jaws.

Why now?

The anguished question stabbed at her.

She picked up her phone. She would text Leon to report that there was still no news. She could not face speaking to him.

Turbid emotion swelled within her, but she dared not let it out. Later—later there would be time. Time to answer the voice that was going round and round in her head.

What happens now to Leon and me? What happens now?

She could not listen to it—yet nor could she silence it.

She stared at her phone screen, steeling herself to text him. Then, before she could do it, she halted. A text was arriving. Instantly everything else went out of her head.

'It's Marika!' she cried out loud.

Her stepmother turned, and her father hurried out of the library.

Ellie read out the text, voice breathless.

Ellie—we're here! We crossed the mountains on foot! Antal met us! Watch the newsfeed! It's amazing! It's why we came!

Frantically Ellie snatched up her tablet, holding it up so her father and stepmother could see. And there on the screen was a sight that told her exactly why her siblings had chosen to get back into Karylya now—a sight that absolutely froze her in disbelief.

It was a live feed from the main town in the southern region of Karylya—a part of the duchy that had always been monarchist. And apparently it still was—or at least pro-Karpardy.

For, there on the town hall balcony, live-streamed, was Marika, standing to one side of Niki. On the other side of her was Antal Horvath. All three were smiling and waving. And above their heads was a banner, held up by the other people now crowding out on to the balcony—a banner that declared the presidential candidacy of Nikolai Karpardy.

Ellie felt her eyes widen in disbelief, and amazement, and another emotion that made her cry out and crush her hand to her mouth.

And as the banner was unfurled, waving in the bright sunshine, a roar went up from the huge crowd the camera had panned round to show, filling the town square to bursting point. The deafening sound of cheering.

Leon stared, mesmerised, watching the same live feed a few moments after Ellie had urgently texted him to do so. Ellie's brother was talking now, addressing the crowd, his Karylyan being simultaneously displayed in English language subtitles.

'I was born and raised to serve my country,' he was saying, his youthful voice clear and ardent. 'That is still my purpose! The only purpose of my life!' His tone changed, his hands reaching out. 'Citizens—my fellow citizens, for I am one of you now!—Karylyans, be loyal to all that our country is and should be! Not a medieval monarchy—nor yet a new dictatorship! But a free democracy! A democracy that must resist tyranny—the fearsome tyranny of a police state—and must have truly free elections!'

With each passionately voiced declaration a roar of cheering went up. And then Antal Horvath, the son of the man who wanted to turn Karylya into a police state, was speaking, too, bewailing his father's ambitions for an uncontested presidency, pledging his support for democracy to Ellie's brother and then taking Marika's hand, telling the still cheering crowd that his heart was hers.

There was yet more deafening cheers and thunderous applause as Niki wrung Antal's other hand and swung it with his into a united triumphant wave, to even greater cheering.

It was masterly—even Leon, with all his cynical worldly wisdom could see that.

The boy's youth—he was barely a legal adult—and his passionate idealism… The young Antal Horvath, only a half a dozen years older than Niki, denouncing his tyrannous father… Mix all that with romantic love—Antal's for Princess Marika—and all of them young and good-looking… People would believe every heartfelt word they said.

Masterly indeed—and incredibly dangerous.

To themselves.

His expression set. Getting Ellie's siblings safely out of Karylya had just become infinitely less likely.

Ellie's brother had declared open defiance—thrown down his gauntlet to the man who had ousted his father. Leon's expression grew grimmer yet. And Matyas Horvath would do everything in his considerable power to crush him.

Ellie was trying to keep her father and stepmother's hopes alive, but the ex-Grand Duke and his Grand Duchess were morbidly fearful. The Karylyan regime had immediately denounced Niki's campaign as illegal, an incitement for monarchist rebellion, and the militia had been despatched to crush it.

As the next days passed the world's media watched with bated breath. This was a news story that had every element to catch the public's attention, from the three young, idealistic and highly photogenic protagonists, to the royal connection, the romantic connection, and Ellie knew with a sinking heart the fact that she herself, with Leon's courting of media coverage of their own wedding and glamorous social life since then, had already made Karylya far more famous than it had been previously.

Ellie cursed herself for more than just that at her sister's naively buoyant texts and obdurately optimistic phone calls, in which she persisted in denying the danger they were in, refusing all her pleas that they flee the country while they could...*if* they could...

Of course we're not running away! Ellie, we know exactly what we're doing! We're saving Karylya! We've been determined to do it ever since Papa was exiled!

Dismay and guilt smote Ellie at her sister's passionate words.

I was so busy with Leon I never noticed what Marika and Niki were planning!

Her heart wrung heavily. But then it seemed she wasn't very good at noticing a lot of things, was she?

Like the way Leon lived in a universe that was as remote from hers as outer space. Cold, lifeless outer space.

She sheered her mind away from that. At least she didn't have to think about it now—didn't have to answer the question that circled endlessly in her head.

What happens now to Leon and me? What happens now? What could happen?

It was impossible—just impossible. Impossible, impossible...

At least she was spared Leon's presence...

* * *

Leon had left Rome immediately after Niki's declaration, heading for Washington to lobby as hard as he could for their rescue, blatantly leveraging his position as Niki's brother-in-law—if not for active support for Niki's candidacy, then for support for his democratic right to run against the man who thought the presidency was his for the taking. Support for Niki's right to safety and condemnation for Matyas Horvath, should he try to crush any opposition to himself.

Then he was back in Europe again, using every contact and acquaintance he'd accumulated in his rise to wealth, pulling every string he could with those bankers and investors to whom a stable and prosperous Karylya was far more valuable than one breaking down into civil strife, potentially even civil war.

The crowds that had initially rallied to Ellie's brother were swelling by the hour, and opposition to Antal's father was mounting daily, now that they had a focus for their protest.

Matyas Horvath had postponed the election and declared a state of emergency, creating sweeping new powers to crush all opposition.

A crisis was clearly looming, Leon thought grimly, emerging from yet another meeting with as many influential financiers as he had been able to muster, having asked them to freeze their investments in Karylya, withdraw all deposits from the Bank of Karylya, sell all their currency holdings and put collective financial pressure on the regime not to be punitive of their ardent new opponents at the risk of destabilising the economy. But what it would be, and when it would strike, he could not say.

He was haunting the Quai d'Orsay in Paris, home of the French foreign office, to garner what news he could from their sources, and had set up similar sources in Berlin, Moscow, Vienna and London's Whitehall. And he had contacts amongst the broadcast media and press, with all their sources of information, as well.

In part of his head he wondered why he was doing it. What was the rest of the Karylyan royal family to him? A sponging ex-Grand Duke and a couple of fecklessly irresponsible younger children…

He thrust the question from his head. He was doing it—that was all.

And when, less than ten days after he'd put Ellie on that plane to Angers, he threw himself into his car and sped out of Paris, he knew exactly why he was doing it.

He arrived at the château as night fell, and strode into the salon, where Ellie and her father and stepmother leapt to their feet, fear instantly on their faces.

'They're safe!' he announced. 'Safer than I ever thought possible.' He took a heaving breath. His eyes wanted only to go to Ellie, but he knew he had to address her father first. 'There has been the most extraordinary development…'

His voice sounded disbelieving even to himself, and if he had not had confirmation of the facts from the French foreign minister himself, and promised to take the news immediately and in person to the ex-Grand Duke, he would not have believed it.

'There's been another coup—Matyas Horvath is under arrest.'

For a second there was complete silence. Then, with a rush, Ellie hurled herself into his arms, clinging to him and bursting into abject tears of relief.

Why was he doing it? Again Leon had his answer.

An answer that within forty-eight hours would turn to ash and bitter cinder in his mouth.

CHAPTER FIFTEEN

LEON STARED AT the television screen in his hotel room above the busy streets of Manhattan. In Karylya it was bright morning—here the dead of night. He took another mouthful of single malt, knowing he should not torment himself by watching, but he could not tear his eyes away.

The ancient medieval cathedral in Karylya's capital was packed, but his eyes were on the figures in the foreground. On one of them only.

Princess Elizsaveta—*his* Princess.

His face contorted, emotion stabbing him and bleakness filling the empty space inside him.

His Princess no longer.

Soon to be his wife no longer.

The bleak words drummed in his head, as they had done ever since he had received her letter, sent from the Karylyan Embassy in Paris, where the Grand Duke and his wife and older daughter had been driven in a chauffeured car flying the royal insignia the moment he'd informed them of the astonishing turn of events in their homeland.

Ellie's letter had arrived two days later.

Dear Leon,

This is to let you know that I am releasing you from our marriage. Thanks to the unexpected events in Karylya, there is no longer any necessity for it.

I wish you well in all your future endeavours, and remain so very grateful for all that you have done for my family, and for our brief time together.

With warmest wishes,

Ellie

He knew it by heart. Every line of it. Every damnable line…

He heard music swelling—the Karylyan Royal Anthem, now being played again in its own land.

The royal family were in exile no longer.

And as the anthem finished he watched the familiar male figure seated on the throne in front of the altar reading out the oath that had been presented to him by his archbishop, his voice resolute.

Watched as the archbishop stepped away and another figure stepped forward, dressed in full ceremonial uniform, ascended the two steps to halt before the throne. He bowed his head and knelt, took the hand of the enthroned man to bestow upon it a kiss of obeisance. He spoke the words of fealty and homage. Straightened and stood aside.

And as he watched something inside Leon rose within him and constricted his throat. An emotion he had thought long destroyed.

The camera pulled back, and now he watched the

Grand Duchess and her stepdaughter and daughter walking forward slowly, with sweeping trains. The three of them were curtsying deeply, the enthroned figure bowing his head regally in acknowledgement.

Leon could watch no more.

He jolted to his feet, snapping off the television set and striding with rapid footsteps into his bedroom, to throw himself down on the bed. His face stark, he stared at the ceiling.

And that long-buried emotion—destroyed so long ago, never to be permitted existence again—forced itself, synapse by synapse, into his head. Widening and growing, strengthening and gaining power...

The power he had denied it for so long. The power he had felt it taking more and more since his marriage. The power that had made him want to unite his life with the woman he had married...the power that had savaged him with fear when she'd wanted to risk her freedom for the sake of her siblings. The power that had devastated him when she'd left him.

The power which now broke from its life-long chains to sear across his heart.

His hands clenched at his sides as it took him over, forcing itself upon him, making him face everything he had rejected and denied. Forcing its truth upon him.

He was crying out inside.

She's left me! She's left me and I cannot bear it—I cannot bear it!

And as the words cried out inside him a terrifying realisation swept through him, jolting him upright to his feet.

The blood drained from his face, bleaching his features. Then slowly, so very slowly, words took shape in his head. Words he clung to like a drowning man a raft.

It's not too late.

Not too late to go to her, to tell her—tell her what now blazed in him with a certainty that shook him to his very core.

Ellie sat herself down on the wooden bench in her step-father's apple orchard. The mossed trees were heavy with fruit, and wasps were feasting on the windfalls in the long grass. She had come here seeking only soli-tude, knowing that her mother would take one look at her, when she arrived from Karylya to burst into tears on her bosom, and understand totally that all she could do now was seek refuge like a wounded animal.

She shut her eyes in misery.

At the very moment of her greatest happiness—Leon wanting to make his life with her, she discovering her glorious love for him and having faith that he would re-turn that love—everything had turned to ash and bitter cinders. All she had hoped for, yearned for—thought she had been granted!—had been destroyed. Destroyed utterly...

Every word of the brief letter she had made herself write to Leon burned in her memory. She had said only what she *had* to say—nothing of what she longed to say, what she could never say.

She had set him free.

As she herself could never be.

Because I will love him all my life.

Anguish filled her face.

And it is because I love him that I have set him free!

I must never impose on him what he told me he's never wanted!

A woman's love.

Her love.

She felt her hands move to her lap, clenching together. She had been over this again and again—was still at war with herself. Longing with every fibre of her being to rush to him—to be his wife on any terms, never telling of her love for him.

But how could I live with him, loving him as I do, knowing he will never—can never—love me in return? That he will never want my love at all! It would slay me, destroy me...

She had asked herself that question over and over again in those terrifying days of fearing she might never see her brother and sister again.

What happens now with Leon and me?

The answer had been impossible to face. But now she had. She had faced it—and given him the freedom from an unwanted love that he had never asked for, never sought. And never would.

So I can never see him again. Never will see him again.

Anguish and loss—tearing, unbearable loss—pierced her like a sword.

A sound came from the top of the orchard—the creaking iron gate opening. Her head twisted round and up. For a second—just a second—her vision was confused by the dappled sunlight under the trees. Then, with a sudden constriction of her throat, her vision resolved itself and she felt a leap in her heart that was boundless joy. And agonising pain.

It was Leon.

* * *

Leon paused, stilling as Ellie's head lifted jerkily and she saw him there. He saw something flare in her eyes—something that speared through him like a fire-tipped arrow. Then it was gone, and all that was in her face was wariness and withdrawal.

He felt emotion stab in him, and then, with determined resolve, he headed through the long grass towards her.

'I need to talk to you.'

Something moved in her face, but she did not speak.

Ellie was incapable of speech. Her senses were drumming with his presence, her heart leaping—but she crushed it back.

Her eyes clung to Leon's face. There was something different about it—his features were etched starkly, tension in every line of him. He sat himself down heavily on the end of the wooden bench, turning towards her. Emotion surged within her, yet still she leashed it back.

'Why?' The single word fell from her lips.

Something flashed in his face, his eyes.

'Why?' he echoed.

Something in Greek broke from him and then, as if getting control back over himself, he leant forward, his hands clasping each other on his thighs. Absently she noticed the muscled power beneath the smooth material of his trousers, noticed the way his knuckles were whitening with the strength of his grip.

'That is *my* question!' he shot at her. '*Why* are you divorcing me?'

He drew breath heavily, his chest rising and falling

in a way that made her eyes cling to him. Faintness was washing through her…emotions were churning through her. To see him again like this, when she had thought never to see him again…

He was speaking again, more words bursting from him.

'Is it just because your father can now afford to repay everything I spent on him, including buying the château? I told you, Ellie!' There was vehemence in his voice. 'I couldn't care less about bankrolling him—or not bankrolling him! That *cannot* be the reason you're ending our marriage!'

His expression changed, became still, and now there was self-condemnation in his voice.

'Is it because I was such a brute when you were trying to go to your sister and brother in Karylya? Threatening to evict your father?' He took another breath. 'I said it only to force your hand! To protect you from yourself! I would never have gone through with it—'

She was shaking her head. Wishing, as she did so, that she could clutch at what he'd said and give him the reason he had come here to find.

The real reason she could never give him.

Because to explain why I have left him will be to place the burden of that reason upon him.

'Then *why*?'

His question came again. His dark eyes rested on her like weights she could not bear—but must.

'I have to know—' He broke off. Shut his eyes a moment.

Ellie's gaze went to his long, dark lashes, brushing

the tanned skin of his cheeks. Emotion washed through her again, weakening her when she must stay strong.

'It is because...' she said slowly, knowing he wanted—needed—an answer, an explanation. 'Because I know I cannot be honest with you. And honesty...' Her voice changed, twisted. 'Honesty is what you value above everything. The only foundation for a marriage.'

A sound broke from him.

'Honesty?'

The derision in the word was infinite. Scathing.

Ellie felt her face blench, the blood draining from it. Dear God—did he know? Had he guessed? Please, no! *No!* She could not bear it—could not bear to place upon him the burden of her love...a burden he did not want—would never want.

But Leon's stark features were twisting again...

'There was nothing *honest* in what I said to you. Nothing!' His jaw set. He felt as if a vice was clamping his throat. 'There was only—' He forced the words out of the depths of his being into the light of day. 'Only fear.'

She stared at him, not understanding. He saw the blankness in her eyes—those beautiful, expressive eyes whose merest glance could stop the breath in his body. Longing filled him, and an ache for her that was a tearing hunger—a hunger for her that had driven him across the Atlantic, to seek and find her...to tell her what he was now telling her. What he must tell her—must face.

The truth he must face himself.

Whatever it cost him to tell her.

He tore his gaze from her, turned his head aside, unable to bear looking at her, longing for her.

He looked, instead, back down the years.

Unconsciously his shoulders hunched, as if he were protecting himself…

Protecting myself from the cold of the Athens winter. My hands thrust into my jeans pockets, my jacket too thin to keep me warm, the soles of my feet freezing as I stand for so long in the queue for the soup kitchen, to fetch the meal I need to take to my mother.

He felt his thoughts shear away, as if an insect had flown too near an open flame and would burn to a frazzle in the space of a second.

'Fear,' he said again.

His gaze lowered, dropped to the sun-dappled grass beneath his feet. The late summer warmth embraced him. A world away from that bitter Athens winter.

His voice, when he spoke, was stark.

'I've told you—have made no secret of it—how bad things were when I was a teenager. How I was left to look after my mother.' His voice hardened unconsciously, as it always did, when he thought of his father abandoning his wife, deserting his family, taking the selfish, uncaring, cowardly way out of a situation he had not wanted to face. 'I did the best I could—'

His voice broke off and for a moment he could not speak, and when he did he felt a bleakness that ripped the very soul from his body.

'I did the best I could,' he said again.

His eyes rested on the lush orchard grass, where a wasp was busy with a fallen apple, but it was not that he saw. It was himself, carrying the metal dish of thick soup, hugging the loaf of bread that had been doled out to him, hurrying up the dirty staircase to the dingy one-roomed flat where he and his mother had to live, their former spacious apartment long gone.

He saw himself opening the door, calling to his mother that he was back, that he'd brought hot food for her.

But she had not answered him.

Had not been able to answer him.

Not then. Nor ever again—

'But it wasn't enough,' he heard himself say now. *'It wasn't enough.'*

A noise came from his throat—a tearing sound. He lifted his gaze, bringing it up to meet the eyes that were resting on him. A light was beginning to form in them that seemed like a mirror of his own. Filling with dread...

'I came back one day from the soup kitchen and found her...found her...'

His fists spasmed, features contorting.

'She'd—she'd cut her wrists. There was blood soaking into the sheets of her bed...so much blood. *So much.* And her face was white—white like the corpse she was. My mother—'

The words were wrenched from him, from the depths of him. From the memory he would never, never allow into his life. The emotion that went with the memory. The emotion he could not bear to feel.

'She left me a note,' he said. 'She said she could not live without the man she loved—my father, who had left her. She could not bear to live without him. So she left me.'

He closed his eyes, screwing them shut so tightly

that the sockets ached. His hands were an agony of clenching.

Pain and grief and loss—unbearable loss—were racking him, and the darkness that filled him, that had always filled him, waited to feed on him, enveloped him as it had that nightmare day.

There was no comfort. No consolation. No way to bear it except the way he had.

Denying love.

Protecting himself from it.

From what it could do.

Had he said the words aloud? He did not know.

But arms were coming around him, around his stricken body…arms were folding him against a body, arms so slight and so slender—so strong. Strong enough to hold him now, as his body shook. And she was cradling him, holding him, saying his name over and over again. He could feel tears on his cheeks, breaking not from the man he was now but from the boy he had once been, too young to bear what had been done to him by a woman who had pitied herself, loved herself more than she had her son, betraying him even as his own father had betrayed him, too.

The arms around him were fast about him now, not letting him go, drawing his head down to her shoulder. She was smoothing his hair as a mother might smooth the hair of her infant, comforting him in her arms. Until at last he felt the racking of his body ebb and was exhausted, spent.

He lifted his head from her shoulder, aware that her hand was enclosed in his, as if he would never let her go. *Could* never let her go.

Ellie was speaking to him. Very slowly, very clearly, her eyes holding his smeared gaze...

'Leon, you must understand me. Just as I now understand you.'

She heard something change in her voice as sudden realisation hollowed her—the realisation of just why he had lashed out so furiously—so condemningly—when she had told him of her sister's despair and her own fear of what it might lead to...

He was remembering his own mother, what her despair did to her, to him...

'Listen to me—*listen* to me.'

She took a breath, impelling him to hear her. To understand. It was the most important thing in the world for him to understand—the most vital thing to make him. Emotion was storming inside her but she could not let it show—horror and disbelief and a pity so profound it wrung her heart.

She spoke again, her voice steady, intent, for he *must* understand this.

'What your parents did to you between them was...' she took another breath '...unforgivable. Your father without a doubt is to be condemned without compunction! But your mother, however great her own misery and heartbreak—' She heard her voice catch, knowing these words were for herself as well as him. 'She should never, *never* have abandoned you the way she did! *No* parent should put their own feelings first!'

These were the words that would show Leon—show that abject, deserted teenager, so cruelly abandoned by the very people who should have been there for him—

that it could be safe to love… That he need not fear love as he did. Need not deny it to protect himself.

Compassion filled her, along with pity and understanding. She lifted her free hand to his cheek, her eyes pouring into his with all that she felt. All that she must show him to make him believe and understand—and trust.

'Your parents failed you, Leon—but not all parents do. Mine have not, for all that they were not happy with each other. And the partners they now have they are truly devoted to. As is my sister to hers, and he to her. And although…' Her voice faltered, but she went on, knowing she must do it for him. 'Although we cannot choose who we fall in love with—or, indeed, out of love with, as your father did your mother, or my parents each other—it doesn't mean we must become slaves to that love, sacrificing our children's happiness to it. We can still make the right moral choices—even if it costs us heartache and heartbreak.'

Just as I, Leon, cannot tell you of my love for you lest it burden you with something unwanted.

And she still could not tell him.

Emotion twisted inside her. Her understanding of Leon now was infinitely greater. Pity and compassion for what he had suffered seared within her. But why should that change anything for her?

'Sometimes, Leon,' she said slowly, 'we have to be brave to love. And one day…' She made the words come, putting into practice what she had just said to him about courage, though it cost her to do it. 'One day you will meet a woman you can love without fear—on whom you can bestow the heart that you have protected so desperately since your parents abandoned you, each in their own disastrous, self-obsessed way, to make the choices they did. I wish that for you, Leon, with all my heart—'

She broke off. It was impossible to say more. Impossible.

Is this the one gift I can give him out of my love for him? To set him free not just from me but from the fear that has imprisoned him all his life? Free to find love.

He was looking at her and his expression was strange. Her hand dropped away from his cheek and suddenly she moved to stand up. She was too close to him—way too close. And for all her brave words she felt her heart contract within her. With love…with pain…

He was getting to his feet as well, still with that expression on his face she had never seen before. But suddenly it seemed to stop the beating of her heart. He stood in front of her but made no attempt to touch her, or close in on her.

His eyes were searching as he spoke. His voice low.

'And what if I told you that I have already found her?' he said, and there was something in his voice that she had never heard before. 'Found the woman I love.'

He paused, and something shifted in his eyes.

'The woman who is already my wife,' he said.

She heard him, but did not hear him. Her gaze could only hold his, uncomprehending. She did not dare to understand. To believe…

He was talking again—and now she heard him. Heard every word.

'It's why I came here,' he said, with that same low, intent tone in his voice. 'To tell you why I said such things to you that night in Rome. To tell you how great a lie they were—to tell you the truth of what I feel for you. What I will always feel. What I started to feel right from the moment of our first incredible night together, though I could not recognise it. A kind of…of *thawing*…as if something frozen deep within me was starting to melt. I felt it again and again—most of all in Puglia, when I knew I wanted to spend my life with you, to make a home with you.'

He took a breath and his voice changed, became edgy.

'I came to tell you of my fear for you—fear that knifed me in my guts—when you said you wanted to risk imprisonment by trying to rescue your brother and sister and I thought I might lose you for years. To tell you of the pain I've felt since you told me our marriage was over. My fear that I'd lost you for ever—just as I lost both my parents—showed me that truth. Showed me so strongly that I could deny it, flee from it, no longer.'

Leon paused, and then he said the words he had come to say.

'The truth is that I love you with all my heart and being—my most beautiful, wonderful Princess, my most beautiful, wonderful woman, my most beautiful, wonderful wife—the love of my heart and my soul.'

He stopped, felt his throat tightening so that he could hardly speak, yet still he knew he must. He could read nothing in her face—nothing in her eyes. But in his head he heard the words she had just spoken to him.

Sometimes we have to be brave to love.

He felt emotion twist in him. Well, he was being brave now—and he must be braver yet.

So he said the final words he must say.

'But if that love is something you do not want I will not burden you with it—'

A cry broke from her. A cry of anguish and heartache. And then tears were spilling from her eyes, from her beautiful, wonderful eyes, and suddenly she was in his arms and words were coming from her in a cry.

'Leon, I want your love with all my heart! For I love you with all my heart! Being without you has been agony—I've missed you so much! I left you, forced myself to leave you, because I didn't want to burden you—'

He did not let her finish her echo of his own words. Words that were cast to the wind now. He swooped his mouth upon hers and as he kissed her felt her cheeks wet with tears. Tears of joy—only of joy.

Ellie held his face in her hands as his mouth released hers, her eyes pouring into his. Joy and thankfulness filled her—not just for herself, but for him, the man she loved, so grievously wounded by the very people who should have protected him. He had found a way to pass beyond what had been done to him. To come to believe that love could be true—that he could risk loving another human being.

And this time—oh, *this* time that love would never be betrayed.

'I will love you always, Leon. Always!' she vowed.

His gaze poured into hers, burning with all that he felt. All that he was now free to feel. And to tell to the woman he loved who, miracle of miracles, returned that love...

His heart overflowed with it.

'And I you,' he said. 'I love you, my one and only love, my beloved wife, my beautiful, peerless princess bride—and I am your liegeman for all time.'

He took her hands, pressing them with his, leading her to sit down on the wooden bench again.

'Your liegeman,' he said again, and lifted each hand to his mouth in homage and in love.

Then he tucked them both into his, holding them fast. He smiled down at her.

So much was in his heart, soaring and swooping, but he had one more thing to say to her. One more wound to heal. For one day, God willing—and he felt his heart soar again even at the very thought that this most precious woman in the world, the woman he loved with all his heart and soul and being, might one day bear a child for him—he must be the father his own had not been to him. The father he could be—*would* be. For now he had proof that such a thing was possible.

'If you want to know,' he said, his voice half-wry, half-serious, 'when it was that I first brought myself to believe that I did not have to perpetually distrust the very concept of love, it was when I was watching the live broadcast from the cathedral. It was seeing your father—'

He broke off. A faint frown creased his brow and his gaze flickered out across the dappled orchard.

'I never liked your father,' he said abruptly. 'I despised him. Like my father, he put himself first. He was willing for his daughter to marry the man—a complete stranger to her—who was paying for his comfortable exile.'

Words of protest rose to Ellie's lips. 'Leon, he was

ashamed of relying on you, and was doing so only for his wife and children's sake! That's why I let him think I'd fallen for you in a *coup de foudre*!' she exclaimed. 'It made it easier for him.'

'Conveniently so,' Leon said tightly. Then his expression changed. 'But all my contempt for him evaporated in that single moment when I saw him in the cathedral. It…it showed me how…how unselfish a father could be—as mine was not. Watching your father do what he did for the sake of someone more important to him than himself—'

'Paying homage to his own son—his sovereign now?' Ellie finished for him. She took a breath. 'He did so, Leon, with all his heart, and such pride in Niki! I promise you—as did we all. That coup which removed Matyas Horvath wanted to restore the monarchy—but not the monarch. And we welcomed it with absolute thankfulness. It was the best possible outcome once the Council had come to see Horvath as a liability. Although…' she looked straight at Leon '…they were helped in that regard by all the lobbying you did, both politically and financially, for which we are all deeply grateful.'

Her expression changed as she went on.

'If there was any concern it was that my father abdicating in favour of his own son would place a burden on Niki that he is very young to take on. But the Council has been incredibly supportive, as you know. Niki will study at Oxford, as was always planned, and get his degree, and as well as attending a monthly Council meeting he will spend his vacations in Karylya, learning the craft of sovereign politics.' She made a wry face. 'My only royal sisterly fear is that he might remember with too great a fondness those heady days when he ran as candidate for a republican presidency!

'But of course,' she went on musingly, 'it was the very fact that he had shown himself so courageous, so idealistic, in risking imprisonment or worse at Horvath's hands, by returning to Karylya at so dangerous a time for him, that so impressed not only the populace but the Council as well. Hence the compromise, which all Karylyans must hope will work for this generation and the future—that my father stands down, of his own free will, and lets his son ascend the throne, calling for fresh elections to a newly created national assembly and instituting a reformed constitution that promotes a more redistributive tax system and gives a fair and just representation to all ethnicities within Karylya.'

'And your sister? What will she do?' Leon raised an eyebrow.

'Well, with Antal's father having now taken himself off out of the country—with a generous pay-off insisted upon by Niki, I might add, who has already learned the wisdom of political clemency to neutralise opposition—Antal is starting his own career: standing as a pro-royalist but reforming candidate in the elections. As for my sister—she and her mother are totally absorbed in planning Marika's wedding...'

She paused, looking at Leon. Her expression changed again. Lightened.

'Will you be my plus one?' she asked.

There was a glint of humour in her eye. And an answering glint in his.

'All your life,' he said. 'For everything. I am your own true liegeman for all time.'

She lifted her face to his. Lifted her heart to his. The heart that was singing with a rapture she had never dared to hope could be hers.

But it is—it is mine, all mine, for all time!

Joy streamed through her—and wonder and elation. She had always yearned to marry for love—and now she had.

And so had Leon. Free to love at last.

As his mouth lowered to hers one thought and one soaring emotion filled her.

So have we both.

And then all conscious thought was lost in the bliss of their embrace.

EPILOGUE

THE DRAWING ROOM in the château on the Loire was bathed in early summer sunshine as Ellie and Leon, newly arrived from their Elizabethan country house in Somerset, purchased just before Christmas, stood in front of the ornate fireplace, smiling at the assembled company.

'My whole family,' said Ellie happily.

They were all there—her parents and their spouses, her half-siblings and her new brother-in-law—and she beamed at all of them.

'We have, as you may well have guessed, an announcement to make,' Leon said.

His voice was warm, and he slipped Ellie's hand into his, throwing her a loving glance which she returned.

Then his gaze went out over the faces smiling back at him. *His* family, too. His mother-in-law, Lady Connie—who was, he knew, overjoyed at their loving happiness—had a fondly expectant look in her eyes that told Leon she had already guessed what he and Ellie's announcement was going to be, and couldn't wait to hear it.

Her husband was stooping to greet the handsome

and usually irascible Pomeranian newly acquired by Ellie's stepmother, which under Malcolm's experienced approach was being far more friendly.

Leon made a mental note to consult his wife's step-father after dinner—Ellie had recommended they ask Malcolm about the mountain nature reserve in Kary-lya that he was financing, one of the new young Grand Duke's enthusiastically promoted schemes for his country.

Another was the new national ballet school, of which the newly-wed Princess Marika was patroness along with the opera house, having taken over that role from her mother.

Her young husband, Antal, now an elected member of the National Assembly, was a junior minister for the arts, with a particular brief for the promotion of traditional crafts amongst the myriad ethnicities in the country, and he was organising an annual cultural festival to celebrate Karylya's diversity.

As for the young Grand Duke himself... Leon could not prevent his lips twitching in amusement at the memory of his arrival, flying in from Oxford for the weekend. Ellie had rushed forward to hug him, only to be brought up short by her stepmother's shocked exclamation.

'Elizsaveta, you forget yourself!'

Dutifully Ellie had halted, dipping down into the required curtsy before her sovereign.

'Not *nearly* deep enough, sis!' her brother had reprimanded pompously, in exaggeratedly lofty tones—which had promptly earned him a thump on his chest and the tart observation that he looked hungover after what had doubtless been a heavy session out clubbing with his university mates the night before.

Niki's parents, once Princess Elizsaveta had acknowledged her brother's sovereignty, had, to Leon's surprise, looked on indulgently—both at the irreverent sibling banter and at the thought of the Grand Duke of Karylya carousing with his fellow students.

But then, Leon thought, everything about the former Grand Duke and Duchess and their new, far more relaxed attitude to life was surprising to him.

Ellie had explained it to him. 'My father never *enjoyed* being Grand Duke,' she'd told Leon. 'To him it was his duty, but always a difficult one. Now that the baton has passed to Niki—who, as is already evident, looks set to make a highly successful go of his reign, for he's wildly popular as my father never was—my father and stepmother are actually much happier. They've genuinely come to love the château you installed them in, now that it's their own. My father's filling the library with his precious rare editions—and he's been invited to remain a patron of the national collection in Karylya, which has pleased him no end—while my stepmother is busy restoring the château's gardens, preparatory to launching an open-air summer opera season in the grounds next year. Oh, and be warned: now that Marika's left home she's got herself a dog! It yaps!'

Now, as Malcolm straightened up, said animal gave a yap of indignation at being deprived of attention and trotted across to his owner, who scooped him up with a doting, 'Up you come, Chou-Chou!', cooing to him fondly in German and urging him to be good because an important announcement was about to be made.

Leon caught her exchanging knowing glances with her predecessor, who nodded as if in confirmation of what both of them were pretty sure they were going to hear.

Well, he would keep them waiting no longer.

'Thank you all so much for coming here,' he opened, smiling at Lady Connie and Malcolm, then at Princess Marika and Antal, 'and, of course,' he went on, 'to my wife's sovereign, for dragging himself away from his studies...' He cast a conspiratorial grin at Niki, who returned it shamelessly, if a trifle blearily. 'Most of all, and it goes without saying...' he inclined his head to the Grand Duke Emeritus and the Grand Duchess Emerita '...to their Royal Highnesses for their hospitality this evening.'

He had married a princess and royalty was royalty.

'A pleasure,' his father-in-law assured him, his tone genial.

Leon drew breath. 'So, I shall hesitate no longer in telling you what I suspect is no secret for some of you...'

His gaze swept over Ellie's mother and stepmother, as well as encompassing Marika, who was whispering something in an excited fashion to her husband.

His gaze came back to Ellie. 'You tell them,' he invited.

Ellie's eyes gleamed and her hand squeezed Leon's. 'We're having a baby!' she exclaimed.

Her mother surged forward. 'Darling, I *knew* it!'

Her hug was tight, her delight warm. Then Marika was hugging her, too, and even her stately stepmother, after handing Chou-Chou to her husband, issued forward to bestow a careful but pleased kiss upon Ellie's cheek.

The former Grand Duke got a protesting yap for his pains, so that he hurriedly set the small dog down on the floor, where it skidded excitedly around on the parquet floor, yapping madly, picking up the excitement of the assembled company.

'My dear, I am so happy for you both!' Ellie's stepmother informed her smilingly.

Her father was shaking Leon's hand in congratulation, and then he was wrapping Ellie in a paternal embrace.

'My darling daughter—'

There was a choke in his voice and Ellie could hear it.

For her ears alone he spoke on. 'My gratitude to you, for what you did—'

She knew what he was referring to, and would let him say no more.

'Oh, Papa, it's all worked out so wonderfully, blissfully well! I love Leon so much! And he loves me! And now...' It was her voice's turn to choke with emotion. 'Now there'll be a baby as well. For all of us.'

'When's it due?' Marika was there now, eagerness in her voice. 'And what are you going to call him or her? Can I be godmother?'

'Autumn... Don't know yet, but there are heaps of names to choose from on our side of the family! And, yes, of course, I'd love you to be godmother!' Ellie laughed.

'If you're having a baby...' Niki's interjection was speculative, his expression even more so '...you can't possibly fit a baby seat in that car of yours, Leon. So you might as well—'

'No way,' said Leon firmly. 'No way am I going to hand it over to you to smash up!'

'As if!' Niki was indignant.

'You can drive it over the weekend—*if* you stay sober!' Leon told him with a half-laugh that got an exclamation of thanks from his brother-in-law. 'By the way,' he prompted the young Grand Duke, 'you should talk some more to Malcolm while he's here…about the nature reserve you want to set up.'

Diverted, Niki sauntered off to intercept the renowned naturalist who was once more practising his dog-calming skills on an over-excited Chou-Chou.

Leon turned to Ellie. Staff were circulating now, serving the celebratory champagne that his father-in-law had summoned, and he took two glasses, drawing her aside a little now her family had let them be.

'One sip won't hurt,' he said, and smiled.

Ellie hoped he was right. It would be the last she could indulge in for quite some time.

She gave a sigh of pleasure at the prospect. Happiness filled her from top to toe, bathing the beloved baby she carried in its glow.

Leon raised his glass to hers. Memory plucked at him, of how he had called for champagne the day she'd come to him, telling him she would agree to marry him.

The most blessed day of his life—but he had not known it then.

He knew it now, though, with a thankfulness that shook him.

'To us,' he said to her, his most wonderful, precious princess bride.

* * *

'To all three of us,' Ellie answered, her hand sliding protectively over where their baby lay, so loved, so precious.

As Leon was to her, and she to him.

'And to our child we will be what your parents were not to you,' she said, her voice low and filled with a certainty, a reassurance, that she knew he needed to hear. 'And oh, Leon…' her voice changed '…who knows? Perhaps, just as it was for my own father, it was shame at his failure to provide for you that made yours do what he did?'

Her eyes searched his.

'Since both of us have experienced the heartbreak of thinking ourselves parted for ever from each other can that not make us a little kinder to your mother, in her despair?' Her expression changed. 'I do not—cannot—condone either of them for abandoning you, each in their separate, heartless way, but—'

'"To understand all is to forgive all"?' Leon finished for her.

His expression was sombre, and there was something in it that she had not seen before. It warmed her to see it there.

'We are so blessed, Leon, you and I—so blessed! Perhaps we should be generous…'

He kissed her softly. 'With you beside me, I can be,' he said. 'With you beside me I can be anything!'

Her eyes clung to his. 'Be the man I love,' she said. 'That is all I ask of you—all I will ever ask of you!'

She kissed him softly. Her strong, wonderful, beloved husband.

Then she clinked her glass to his, and he clinked his to hers, and they drank to the baby that awaited the most loving parents ever...

* * * * *

Wrapped up in the drama of
The Greek's Duty-Bound Royal Bride?
Dive back into Julia James's passionate world with these other stories!

Tycoon's Ring of Convenience
Heiress's Pregnancy Scandal
Billionaire's Mediterranean Proposal
Irresistible Bargain with the Greek

Available now!

#3805 THE SPANIARD'S SURPRISE LOVE-CHILD
Passion in Paradise
by Kim Lawrence

Softhearted Gwen had always dreamed of the day tycoon Rio would discover their child. Yet the reality is astounding! Because when the brooding Spaniard sweeps back into her life, he demands their daughter—and her!

#3806 MY SHOCKING MONTE CARLO CONFESSION
Passion in Paradise
by Heidi Rice

He's Monaco racing royalty and I, Belle Simpson, was his housekeeper. But that evening, Alexi's searing gaze exhilarated me. Five years later, I finally have the chance to reveal my secret—Alexi's a father!

#3807 A BRIDE FIT FOR A PRINCE?
Passion in Paradise
by Susan Stephens

Samia's thrilled by the longing Prince Luca awakens within her but knows a temporary fling is their only option. A future with him is impossible. For the shadows of her past make Samia wholly unsuitable...don't they?

#3808 A SCANDAL MADE IN LONDON
Passion in Paradise
by Lucy King

Kate is *mortified* when billionaire Theo discovers her secret dating profile. Yet she can't resist his tantalizing offer to introduce her to pleasure beyond her wildest imagination! But the biggest scandal of all is yet to happen...

_____

HPCNMRB0320

SPECIAL EXCERPT FROM

H HARLEQUIN

PRESENTS

Theo has one goal: vengeance on his runaway bride, Helena! But Theo can't escape the past...or the intense connection that spectacularly reignites between them. Will this tycoon be tempted to rewrite the rules of his revenge?

Read on for a sneak preview of
Michelle Smart's next story for Harlequin Presents
His Greek Wedding Night Debt

Did she realize that every time she spoke to him, she tilted toward him? Did she realize that she fidgeted her way through every conversation? Was she aware that her breath hitched whenever he walked past her? Was she aware that at that very moment her hands trembled?

"The next thing I wanted to discuss is the kitchen," she said, moving the conversation on.

"What about it?" he asked lightly.

She tugged at the sheets of paper he'd placed his backside on. "You're sitting on my notes."

"My apologies." Sliding smoothly off the desk, he went and sat on the chair on the other side of her desk. "Is this better?" But she didn't respond. Her eyes were on his, wide and stark, her fidgety body suddenly frozen. "Helena?"

She blinked at the mention of her name and quickly looked down at her freed notes.

"Yes. The kitchen." Despite Helena's best efforts, her voice sounded all wrong.

It had been hard enough to breathe with Theo propped on her desk beside her—when he'd first perched himself there, she'd feared her heart would explode out of her chest—but when he'd moved off, she'd had to fist her hands to stop them from grabbing hold of him. Now he was sitting opposite her and she'd caught a sudden glimpse of his golden chest beneath the collar of his polo shirt, and in the breath of a moment her insides had turned to mush.

It shouldn't be like this, she thought despairingly. She'd spent three months under Theo's intoxicating spell, riding the roller coaster of her life.

He'd had the ability to make her forget everything that mattered. Under his spell she'd believed all she needed was Theo in her life to be happy. She was sure her mother had once believed the same thing before she'd sold her soul to a monster. Theo wasn't a monster like Helena's father, but his power over Helena had been just as strong.

How could she still react so strongly to him? She'd believed the sudden detonation of their relationship had killed her feelings for him, but she saw now that she'd been hiding them, hiding them so deep inside that she'd forgotten how powerful they were until one look at him in the Staffords boardroom had seen them poke their heads out from dormancy. Now the old feelings were slapping her in the face, taunting her, and it was getting harder and harder to fight them.

Eyes now determinedly fixed on the papers on her desk, she rubbed the nape of her neck, cleared her throat and tried again. "We need to discuss the kitchen's layout. Do you still want to consult a professional chef about it?"

She knew the moment she said it that she'd made a mistake.

Something sparked in his eyes. He leaned forward a little, a satisfied smile spreading over his face. "You do remember."

"Only that neither of us can cook." She quickly fixed her gaze back on her notes, aware her face was flaming with color.

"But you asked—specifically—if I still wanted to consult a chef about the kitchen… What else do you remember?"

She tucked her hair behind her ear and wrote something nonsensical on her notepad. "Have you a chef in mind to consult?"

"Answer my question."

Her hand was shaking too much to write anything else.

"Helena."

"What?" Helena intended for her one-syllable question to come out as a challenge. She might have succeeded if her voice hadn't cracked.

"Look at me," he commanded.

Heart thrashing wildly, she breathed deeply before slowly raising her face. "What?"

His voice dropped to a murmur. "What do you remember?"

Trapped in his stare, she found herself unable to lie. "Everything."

Don't miss
His Greek Wedding Night Debt
available April 2020 wherever
Harlequin Presents books and ebooks are sold.

Harlequin.com

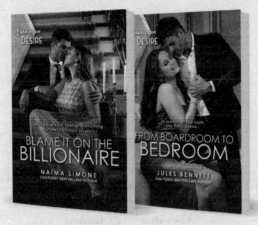

26061

Love Harlequin romance?

DISCOVER.

Be the first to find out about promotions,
news and exclusive content!

 Facebook.com/HarlequinBooks

Twitter.com/HarlequinBooks

Instagram.com/HarlequinBooks

Pinterest.com/HarlequinBooks

ReaderService.com

EXPLORE.

Sign up for the Harlequin e-newsletter and
download a free book from any series at
TryHarlequin.com

CONNECT.

Join our Harlequin community to
share your thoughts and connect
with other romance readers!
Facebook.com/groups/HarlequinConnection

 **HARLEQUIN**